THE
PUTNAMS
OF
SALEM

A Novel of Power and Betrayal
During the Salem Witch Trials

GREG HOULE

Blydyn Square Books

Kenilworth, New Jersey

© 2024

This is a work of fiction. Names, characters, places, and incidents are either the product of the author's imagination or are used fictitiously. Any resemblance to actual persons, living or dead, events, or locales, is entirely coincidental.

CIP information available upon request.

All rights reserved. The scanning, uploading, and electronic sharing of any part of this book without the permission of the publisher constitutes unlawful piracy and theft of the author's intellectual property. If you would like to use material from the book (other than for review purposes), prior written permission must be obtained by contacting the publisher at info@blydynsquarebooks.com.

Cover design by: Michael Helou
Interior design by: Gram Telen

For my mother—a Putnam who has always believed in me

Author's Note

The story of the Salem witch trials has been told and retold many times over, in a variety of ways—from nonfiction and fiction books to short stories, from plays and films to art and dance. It's a tale that has taken on a life of its own. The witch hysteria in Salem has been used as the basis for allegory as well as for punchlines, and for everything in between. Yet none of what it has become over the past three centuries can erase the reality of what happened in and around Salem, Massachusetts, in 1692. I wanted to tell this story—in novel form—as a means for sparking curiosity about why the Salem witch hysteria took place at all. Though there is much we will never know about these events, I believe exploration can help us get closer to the truth. And getting closer to the truth is important. After all, those who cannot remember the past are condemned to repeat it.

The narrators I chose to use for this novel are a father and daughter who played key roles in these events. Thomas Putnam Jr. was forty years old when the witch hysteria struck. The patriarch of a once great but fading family, he saw himself as a pillar of the community. His oldest daughter, Ann, often known as Anna, was twelve at the time, an adolescent trying to make her way in an increasingly complex world, burdened with a distracted father and an emotionally distressed mother. Each of them provides a unique vantage point from which to tell this gruesome piece of early American history. Thomas was one of the most prolific accusers of witches, while Anna was among those who were said to be "afflicted" by so-called witches. In many ways, the two appear to occupy opposite ends of the spectrum—one doing battle against supposed evil and the other tormented by it—yet Thomas and Anna also seemed to be working in concert with each other.

The Putnams are certainly compelling narrators for a story about the Salem witch trials, but there is another reason I chose to tell this story from their point of view. As it happens, their story is also a part of my own. Thomas is my seventh great-grandfather on my mother's side, and Anna is my sixth great-aunt. Like my seventeenth-century ancestors, I was born and raised in New England. I moved away right before my eighteenth birthday without ever having taken much interest in the events in Salem, despite the family lore that linked me to them and my lifelong passion for history. I can't put my finger on my apathy, exactly. It might have been because I thought that the Salem witch trials seemed to be overblown or somehow unworthy of my attention. It seemed that the witch hysteria in Salem had become less about history and more about ghost stories.

Nonetheless, everything changed during the summer of 2021. That August, while visiting family, I took a day trip from Boston to Salem with my wife, Joanna, and my then twelve-year-old daughter, Addison. It seemed like a fun way to spend a Saturday and an opportunity to help Addy, who also has an interest in history, connect with her ancestry and its own role in this terrible American story. But our visit seemed to spark something in me, and I began to look with increasing fascination at my Salem ancestors: this father-daughter duo who helped inflame an infamous tragedy. I began to imagine what must have been going through each of their minds during those frenetic months when the whole region seemed to be combusting uncontrollably. What were they thinking about? What did they talk about? What did they hope to accomplish? We will never truly know the answers to these questions with certainty, of course. But like anyone with an interest in history, I became enthralled by them, nonetheless. I felt compelled to explore them and bring them to life through my own writing.

More than anything else, I quickly came to learn that the events that took place in and around Salem in 1692 were about much more than the collective response of some frightened Puritans to suspected witchcraft. Their concerns were strikingly similar to what human beings have grappled with for centuries and continue to grapple with today: a fear of the other and the unknown, as well as a desire to hold onto power and privilege at all costs. The witch hysteria in Salem was an unmitigated tragedy. Twenty-five innocent people needlessly lost their lives because of it, and nineteen were convicted by a court and executed. But the motivations behind this tragedy should seem familiar to us, even more than three centuries later.

This novel wouldn't exist without the support and love of many people. I am particularly grateful to everyone at Blydyn Square Books for taking a chance on an unknown, first-time author. I am particularly indebted to the talents of my editor, Tara Tomczyk, whose efforts and thoughtful suggestions greatly improved the novel. Professor Kathleen Brown, a fine historian at the University of Pennsylvania, generously offered her time and considerable illuming insights. I also owe much to Ashley Murphy, the editor of *Sundial* magazine, for publishing some early and much different short stories based on this idea. I also want to acknowledge the hard work of countless scholars, researchers, and archivists who have collected and curated an abundance of records and information about the Salem witch trials that I was able to tap into—in particular, the Salem Witch Trials Documentary Archive at the University of Virginia as well as the trove of information provided by the Salem Witch Museum in Salem, Massachusetts. These resources, and many others, proved to be indispensable as I re-created the setting and chronology of this world.

To be clear, *The Putnams of Salem* is a work of fiction. Though the setting, chronology of events, and characters in the novel generally follow the reality of what happened, most of what is written comes from my own imagination because it is impossible to know exactly what Thomas and his daughter Ann were thinking during those fiery months in 1692. If you are interested in learning more about the history of this remarkable period of early American history, I implore you to read the excellent work of the numerous historians and writers who have researched and written about it, including Carol Karlsen, Emerson Baker, Mary Beth Norton, Stacy Schiff, and many others. You will not be sorry that you did.

I would not have been able to write *The Putnams of Salem* without the love and support of my wife, Joanna. Her encouragement, careful evaluations, and thoughtful questions helped me greatly improve my writing, and I am enormously grateful for her willingness to lovingly endure many conversations about what was in my head. She is my partner in every way, and I cannot imagine being on this journey without her. I am also grateful to my daughter, Addy, who humored me by reading an early version of the novel. Her love and encouragement have always been a driving force for me. I cannot possibly be prouder of the person she is becoming. She is my greatest treasure.

Finally, I would not be here at all without my wonderful parents, Gloria Putnam Houle and David Houle. Their everlasting love and support have meant so much to me.

Greg Houle
Los Angeles
August 2023

Prologue

I hate how Betty holds the egg. She makes such a show of it, covering it up entirely with her hand and fingers and presenting it before us like some kind of precious jewel. She acts as if that egg matters more than anything else in the world. Her cousin Abby is stretched out with her eyes closed and the slightest bit of a smirk upon her mouth, ready to receive her future. We are in our usual location in the forest, well hidden from view.

Yet it is all so frivolous, to say nothing of its immorality. If Betty's father found out, we would all be in serious trouble. And Reverend Parris would forever view us differently. It is a fate too unbearable to contemplate. Yet I must participate in this game, despite the danger. I am afraid I am far too concerned about what Betty thinks of me. That is why I am here.

Betty is always eager to talk about it. She wants us all to understand that the most critical part of fortune-telling is one's ability to properly deliver the question from one's mind, through the arm and hand, past the shell, and into the egg white itself, which is then to be dropped into the water to reveal its secrets. If just one of these connections is broken, she tells us solemnly and with a seriousness that seems contrived, then the reading will be entirely faulty. Betty says that it takes great concentration to make these connections and that only a truly powerful person can manage such a thing.

"What profession will my future husband have?"

Abby asks the question—it is the same question we all ask—of nobody in particular. Of course, none of us wants to be the wife of a beggar or a grave-digger, but I wish I could ask a different question. Am I going to heaven? Am I on God's chosen path? These are the answers I wish to know.

We call it the Venus Glass, but Betty prefers to use the strange word, oomancy, when she is introducing it to somebody new, always taking extra care to draw out her pronunciation to impress them. She will inevitably tell them that it comes from the ancient Greeks. I am struck by how the reverend's daughter and her cousin never seem to have the slightest concern about getting caught engaging in such an activity. Given their station, I suppose they believe themselves impervious to risk and incapable of sin.

But I will never forget the fear on Betty's face after she dropped the egg white into the glass—it was like nothing I had ever seen before. And I pray to God I will never witness such a scene again.

PART 1

THE HAUNTINGS

CHAPTER 1

SALEM VILLAGE, PROVINCE OF MASSACHUSETTS BAY

FEBRUARY 1692

Do not turn to mediums or seek out spiritists, for you will be defiled by them. I am the LORD your God.
— **Leviticus 19:31**

"Child, follow my finger with your eyes. Can you hear me?"

Dr. Griggs's voice has a sharp edge to it. He is agitated and his face is red with anger—or perhaps it is embarrassment. Abigail and Elizabeth remain impervious to his futile commands. The doctor appears older and more harried than I remember him being. He is an unimpressive and dowdy man whose misplaced irritation only confirms my disdain for his kind.

I ask him if there is anything he can do for the girls, hoping it might focus his attention on some specific purpose. But he waves me off dismissively.

"That is why I am here, Sergeant Putnam."

His words are punctuated by an exasperated sigh. It is best not to press him further, not under these circumstances. Yet any hope I might have once held in his abilities has now gone. I have little use for doctors. I am not convinced of their value, and I avoid them with much determination. Dr. Griggs's actions only validate my own well-formed opinion. Still, I will hold my tongue. I do not wish to challenge him further in front of the reverend, who is already in much distress. I am of little use here, but Reverend Parris sent for me, and I will remain by his side as he has requested.

"Can you hear the sound of my voice, girl?"

Griggs is speaking very loudly at Elizabeth. He seems to be hoping with some obvious desperation that increasing his volume will somehow break through to her. Reverend Parris explained when I arrived about half an hour ago that Elizabeth had been running about the parsonage, frantically screaming. He said she was as wide-eyed and crazed as a girl possessed, and as soon as she heard the doctor's knock at the door, she fell to the ground right where she stood and became entirely incapacitated. That is where she has remained since—breathing steadily, with her eyes open wide. She is listless and vacant, nothing more than an empty vessel, staring into some unknown abyss.

Griggs is fumbling through his kit, searching for solutions, but it seems like only a performance now. He has nothing left to give. He is putting on a show to justify his presence here, and his considerable fee. I can see that Reverend Parris is growing more distraught at the sight of this man's vain flailing, but he has not said anything to him yet. Perhaps the reverend is too unnerved to protest. Perhaps he is expecting me to speak with the doctor in his stead. I choose to restrain myself for now, not wishing to create a worse scene than what we already have before us.

Reverend Parris's niece, Abigail, is peacefully sleeping in her bed. When he collected me, John, the reverend's servant, explained that both girls seem to be similarly vexed. Yet, in contrast to Elizabeth, Abigail appears like a beautiful angel, resting quietly upon her bed. The sight of the two girls makes for a strange juxtaposition: one seemingly in the throes of terror and the other apparently enjoying the bliss of slumber.

As Dr. Griggs continues his futile efforts, I follow the exasperated reverend into the next room, where he goes to remove himself from the dreadful scene. I relish the opportunity to be alone with him, away from the feckless doctor. Placing my hand upon Reverend Parris's back, I take the opportunity to provide him with some reassurance.

"The girls' condition will improve, Samuel," I say. "God will see to it if we put our hopes in Him. You know as well as I—"

"Stop, Thomas!"

The reverend's response surprises me, and for a moment, I am taken aback. I should have known he would be too clever not to see through my attempts at supplication.

"This is a dreadful situation," he tells me with some irritation in his voice, "and nothing you can say to me now will improve upon it. I know you mean well." He gives a slight shake of his head. "But . . ." His quivering voice fades away without finishing his thought.

I understand the reverend better than most do. He is a unique and remarkable man, nothing like those who go about their day in service only to themselves. We are the same in many ways. Both of us recognize the higher purpose that we serve. The reverend is usually quite unflappable. He has not been so easily shaken by our history of provocation and strife. Instead, he manages our petty squabbles with steadfast poise and dignity. I suppose he must be aware of his great blessings and confident that his keen guidance will lead us to our salvation. But he does not display this knowledge outwardly. That is why I am unsettled by his uneasiness now. It is not like him to be moved in such a way.

After a minute or so of silence, I am relieved at the sound of the door opening. I am startled by how grateful I am for the opportunity to turn our attention elsewhere. From the other room, Dr. Griggs shuffles loudly through the door, wearing a confused look and a furrowed brow of concern. His feebleness and ignorance are now fully on display. I flash a quick glance at Reverend Parris, wondering if he is having a similar reaction to the doctor's display, but I can read nothing on his face beyond his ongoing strain and deep concern.

Griggs carefully closes the door behind him and seems to make a conscious effort to collect himself, building suspense with a deep and profound breath that he exhales slowly.

"The evil hand is upon them, Reverend Parris," he says. "I am afraid there is nothing that I can do."

I can hear her steely voice cutting through the wisps of cool air. It is warmer today than it has been, but there is still a bite. Winter has not loosened her grip on us just yet. Tituba's voice is impossibly high, and the melody she sings is haunting and strange. It floats in the air like a moth, bouncing wildly along the contours of the breeze, rising and falling as it reaches my ears. I cannot understand what she is singing; none of us can understand, not even her master, Reverend Parris. But it is unlike anything we have heard before.

Tituba has sung this song before, many times. Perhaps she is doing the washing in the parsonage yard, as she often does. Whether it is in the hazy warmth of summer or the stark frigidity of winter, Tituba sings her melancholy song without the slightest hesitation in her voice. She seems to revel in its odd dissonance. Perhaps it is her testament to us. She is leaving a mark for us to know her by. I admire Tituba's fortitude. She is unafraid to use her most confident voice despite knowing that we will find it strange. Such things seem to be of no concern to her. She is not a shy woman, in spite of the way she presents herself. She tries to follow our customs, mostly, but she does not hesitate to engage in manners that contrast with them entirely.

We say that John Indian is her husband but, in truth, I do not believe they have exchanged vows before God. I suppose it does not matter. Because they are natives, nobody seems to be concerned with what vows they have exchanged, not even Reverend Parris. They are together, and it seems to be all that matters. It is natural for the two of them to be together, and they care for each other like husband and wife, but I do not see tenderness between them.

"How do you fare, my dear?"

Tituba's song is still floating in the air as Goodwife Sibley passes by. I attempt to placate her with a simple nod, but she is too eager to speak to me to allow me to pass without a word.

Goody Sibley, a short and stout woman who sways wildly from side to side as she walks, appears much older than she is. She seems eager to be everywhere at once, even if she finds it difficult to do so. She is hungry to provide her unwanted advice or to lend her ear to any concern, purely for the benefit of what she might gather in the process. She is chief among those in our village who have an insatiable need for news and whispers. Such things are like currency for Goody Sibley—a serious business requiring hard work. The smile she wears does not indicate friendliness. Instead, it reveals her judgment and the unquenchable thirst she retains for rumor and innuendo. Surely, she appreciates the advantage afforded to her by living in such proximity to the parsonage. Perhaps that is why she has developed such an interest in rumor in the first place. Prime access to the most important goings-on in the village has bred the desire within her. There are many here who involve themselves in the affairs of others; Goody Sibley is not alone in this endeavor. But there is none better at it than she. Her scrutiny is often unbearable. She must know what has happened to Abby and Betty, but she seems to want to keep it to herself.

"I am well, Goodwife Sibley," I tell her with my best smile. "And so is my family."

But the words roll off my tongue too quickly and I walk at an accelerated pace, hoping to get away from this woman as fast as I can. Of course, I know I will not be able to placate

Goody Sibley so easily. And I know that she will soon reveal her knowledge to me about Abby and Betty, pressing me hard about what I know of their condition. I want no part in any of it, so I continue my journey as quickly as I can, despite knowing full well I will not be successful.

Goody Sibley remains firmly where I left her. Even though I have turned away from her and am unable to see her directly, I know with certainty that she has stopped where she stood and is now staring intently at me. I am unsurprised when I finally turn to glance back and see her loitering in the same location, clearly weighing what she wishes to say to me before I can get out of earshot.

"I have told John what he should do."

Goody Sibley's harsh whisper strikes me like a sudden rush of wind. It is loud enough for me to hear from where I am standing, several paces away, but still soft enough to be taken as a secret. I do not immediately take her meaning, and she repeats her phrase in response to my inquisitive look, waddling quickly toward me and losing her breath as she speaks.

"About the condition of the girls!" she continues.

Her response now is impatient—almost angry—and in her full voice. It seems she is no longer concerned about trying to conceal what she is saying from anyone who might be listening.

"I told him what needs to be done to make them better. Tituba can make the witchcake. She and John are the only ones who can do such a thing. It is their only hope for knowing what has happened to the girls. The witchcake will reveal it."

Words are now spilling out of Goody Sibley's mouth with breathless abandon. She seems incapable of keeping her thoughts inside for even a moment longer. It is as if a dam has broken. It is not surprising she is meddling in this business, nor is it unusual that she has chosen to strike now, whispering into John's ear about a so-called witchcake, as soon as Reverend Parris left town for a day or two with his wife to preach in the countryside. Goody Sibley loves nothing more than to stir up trouble. It seems to be her primary vocation. Still, I suspect that Tituba is willing to do anything that might offer even the dimmest hope for the girls' recovery. She loves them dearly. Perhaps that is why she is singing her sad song. Perhaps she is soothing herself from the pain of this awful predicament. Perhaps poor Tituba is trying to strengthen her nerve with her song.

As I walk away from Goodwife Sibley, relieved to have finally broken free from her urgent whisperings, I can no longer hear Tituba's song wafting through the cool, crisp air. It seems the parsonage has gone as silent as the grave.

CHAPTER 2

These will go away into eternal punishment, but the righteous into eternal life.
—**Matthew 25:46**

"You understand, Thomas, I had no choice."

Reverend Parris seems discomfited and ill at ease, even while sitting by his hearth in the comfort of the parsonage. His eyes dart about the room uncomfortably, seemingly unable to focus upon me as we talk. Yet his eagerness to speak signals some strong desire within him to discharge his concerns.

"Of course, I understand, Samuel. Your own daughter and niece have been afflicted. We must get to the bottom of this madness. And it is never easy for a leader to dispatch his responsibilities."

I do my best to put him at ease, hoping my words will provide him with some measure of comfort, but it seems that my efforts are achieving little.

"When I returned home from my lecture and saw that, that . . . cake . . ."

The reverend seems to want to use some other word, but he pronounces *cake* with much disdain, as if it were something strange and foreign.

"I knew immediately what it was, Thomas. I am not sure how, but I knew, with every fiber of my being." Reverend Parris pauses for a moment, as if to collect himself, before continuing. "I had feared that this would happen. I knew Goody Sibley would meddle in our business. During the journey home from my lecture, I even told my wife about my fears in this regard. That woman, Sibley, cannot help herself."

The reverend's anger is something I have not seen from him before, a deep-seated and vicious irritation. Like any good pastor, his usual mannerisms lean toward benevolence and magnanimity. I do my best to bring him back to this placid state.

"You were wise to know this," I tell him in a strong and confident voice. "You should take comfort in your knowledge of the workings of this community. You know us well, Reverend."

It seems that he has not heard my response. He continues speaking in his irritated tone as if I have said nothing.

"I also knew that she would turn to Tituba and John. Goody Sibley is a coward, and, because of this, she was always going to command the two of them to carry out her roguish desires."

"Goodwife Sibley is certainly mischievous," I interject, continuing with my mission to soothe the reverend's nerves. "You will get no argument about that from me. But if Tituba is loyal to you, why did she carry out such a command?"

My question is meant to redirect the reverend's building anger away from Goody Sibley and toward Tituba, whom he chose to punish for producing the witchcake. Perhaps I am too sanguine in my belief that this might help justify his actions against her and put his mind at ease, but it seems worth an attempt, nonetheless.

"It was an impulse," Reverend Parris replies. "It was never my desire to strike her—as God is my witness, Thomas, it was not."

After pausing for a few seconds, he continues.

"Perhaps it was that Sibley woman I wished to punish, and Tituba was all that was available to me in that moment," he says with a shake of his head. "But I am not so absent of mercy that I cannot perceive how Tituba might have believed that such a wretched thing might have helped Betty and Abby. Those poor girls."

Reverend Parris turns toward the fire and warms his hands absentmindedly, before pivoting back to me.

"Perhaps my hand was propelled by the glory of God," he says, "but I cannot shirk my own responsibility on this matter."

He seems less anxious now, perhaps relieved to have been able to unburden himself. Regardless of the reason, I attempt to comfort him further.

"No man of principle—nor a man of God—can possibly stand idle before such sinfulness, Samuel," I tell him with a certainty in my voice. "You cannot punish yourself for standing up to such evil."

His eyes suddenly narrow, his anger seemingly manifesting itself once again.

"After I struck her, Thomas, I could see the slightest hint of a smile still upon her lips," he said as he gazed into the middle distance, seemingly unable to make eye contact with me. "I struck her hard, and with my full force, using the back of my hand. I struck her across her mouth, yet that look—that faint, diabolical smile—remained firmly in place."

I am at a loss about how to respond to him.

"It set me alight, Thomas," he continues when I say nothing. "I was suddenly possessed with anger and range like I never have been before. That smile . . ."

He trails off with another shake of his head, and I choose not to respond, still unsure of what I might say that could be of any use.

"I do not mean that I was processed by anything untoward," he says suddenly, as if to make his meaning clearer to me. "I hope you understand. It seemed that I had become a soldier of the Almighty, I suppose. It was as if I had been given my orders to avenge this wickedness and I had set to work to do my duty."

The reverend's face reflects a look of determination, and I seize the opportunity to soothe him as much as I am able to.

"You are a good man, Samuel, a true man of God. You would not be our pastor if this were not the case."

Ignoring my words, the reverend continues to recall his actions against Tituba: "I struck her across the face two or three or perhaps four times, in quick succession. I might have struck her more than that, Thomas. I do not know. I cannot be sure how many times it was."

Again, I find myself unable to find the words to respond in any useful manner, but my silence is irrelevant, as he continues speaking, unabated.

"I struck her until I finally removed that faint smile from her face. She let out a loud cry after I struck her across her face a few times, and she fell back against the wall of her quarters. But I hit her again. Even after she had fallen, I hadn't finished with her yet."

I want nothing more now than to lessen his growing intensity, so I interject, hoping to redirect his attention elsewhere.

"And what about John?" I ask. "What about her husband? Where was he while this was taking place?"

"He was outside of her room. He entered when he heard Tituba's cries. The look in his eyes. It was like nothing I had seen before. But he wisely chose not to make a move against me, and he held his tongue, as well."

I have no difficulty imagining the look upon John's face that the reverend is describing. I have seen such a look before from John's kind, while fighting the natives during the war. The intensity of it can overwhelm. It is not a look of a civilized man.

"John is aware of his position here," I tell the reverend. "He would never do anything to jeopardize what we have given him. He knows better than to act against you."

As before, Reverend Parris appears not to hear my reply. "I do not doubt or regret my actions against Tituba," he tells me. "As you say, it was a just punishment under the circumstances. But I did not wish to have any further part in it. Such messy business is not the duty of a pastor."

"Of course," I say, perhaps a bit too quickly. "You were only doing what needed to be done."

"I ordered John to go to the yard and produce a sturdy switch, which he did with much haste," the reverend continues. "I then commanded him, in a very harsh tone—a tone that I was unaware that I processed—to dispatch his husbandly duties immediately."

I attempt to hide my surprise, but my eyebrows must have betrayed me, as is their wont to do.

"If John wishes to call Tituba his wife," I say, praying my response will ease the reverend's concern, "then he must play the part."

Despite my assurances, the reverend continues, seemingly intent on describing every minute detail.

"I screamed at John and ordered him from the top of my lungs to obey me," he says. "I was like a man processed: 'Strike her! Punish your ill-mannered wife or else you will feel God's wrath!' I dispatched all manner of epithets at him without relent. I am not even aware of everything that I said or did in that moment. It was madness."

It seems best now for me to listen rather than respond; to provide Reverend Parris with the opportunity to unburden himself of his concerns.

"John struck Tituba several times with the hearty tree branch he chose. He struck her hard across her back and shoulders. Tituba screamed out, thunderously bellowing after each lash."

Reverend Parris is speaking now with a more measured firmness. It sounds as if his teeth are clenched as he speaks.

"She appeared to be surprised by John's actions. It was as if she had not expected her husband to punish her in such a manner. She glared at him with much contempt, with tears in her eyes."

"Of course, it is a husband's responsibility to keep order in his family," I respond. "God expects as much from both master and slave."

"I was entirely frozen," Reverend Parris continues. "I could do nothing but witness this brutality play out before me, this punishment I myself had ordered John to carry out upon his own wife."

The reverend's voice seems to break as he says these words, and he pauses for a moment before beginning again.

"I am meant to be compassionate, Thomas," he says, quietly now. "Yet in that moment I was as bloodthirsty as the most savage among us."

He is silent for a long moment. It seems almost as if he is in mourning.

"After John struck Tituba a few more times, he looked up at me with a pleading look in his eyes," the reverend continues. "He was panting loudly, but otherwise he remained entirely silent as he stood before me. Glistening with sweat, he did not utter a single word.

"He was begging me with his eyes, Thomas. John was beseeching me, without uttering even a single syllable, to permit him to stop punishing his wife. Yet I said nothing to him." He sputters impotently, barely able to get the words out of his mouth.

There is nothing for me to say. I must simply remain attentive and listen closely as he speaks. It seems that my role is to be his confessor.

"I am a leader in this community," he finally says, more composed now. "I cannot afford to be so feckless in the face of such circumstances. My responsibilities require decisiveness and certainty, always."

The candid words seem to lead us both into silence for a while. Then, after a few minutes with only the sounds of the fire crackling in the hearth, the reverend begins speaking again, this time in a firm and confident tone.

"Thankfully, God gave me the strength. I had but a moment's hesitation and then I raised my hand and put a stop to the beating. It had been accomplished. Tituba had been punished for her transgression."

"God tests us, Samuel," I say, pleased that the reverend has returned to his usual manner. "And I have no doubt that you are the man that He has chosen for us. We are all grateful that you are here to carry us toward God's light."

Dorothy Good's small, rough hands wrapped firmly around my neck startle me awake. I cannot imagine dreaming of anything more fantastical, but I feel as if I must be having a nightmare when I see her standing before me in the darkness.

"What are you doing?" I attempt to say to the unmistakable form of this small child standing next to my bed, ruthlessly attempting to snuff the life out of me.

"He has told me to kill you, Anna. I must do what he requests."

Dorothy's voice, coarse and ill-formed, hasn't a hint of compassion to it. Although the pressure on my throat is firm, at barely four years old, Dorothy does not yet possess enough strength to close off my air entirely. Still, I struggle mightily to break free from her surprisingly strong grip.

"Why are you doing this to me? Why are you here in my room?"

"It is because of my familiar, Anna," the girl says to me in her raspy, immature voice. "My snake was given to me by Mother, and he speaks to me. He guides me, Anna. He tells me what I must do. He bites me on my finger to give me strength, to give me power."

Upon saying this, Dorothy lets go of my throat and holds out her tiny right forefinger, revealing two small red dots at the base. Despite now being free from Dorothy's grip, I am unable to move, seemingly locked into place by some unknown force.

After a moment of silence and confusion, Dorothy's gaze suddenly refocuses upon me, and she narrows her small, dark eyes. Then, like a rabid animal, the child maneuvers her face close to me and quickly sinks her teeth into my left forearm.

"I am biting you like my snake bites me," she says quickly between bites. Blood appears and starts to drip down the girl's mouth. "I must bite you, Ann Putnam! He has ordered me to do it, so I must!"

Dorothy's teeth feel like sharp pinpricks as she opens and closes her mouth in quick succession, up and down my arm.

"Stop this! Stop this immediately, Dorothy! Why are you doing this to me? Stop!"

My cries go unheeded. Dorothy continues her assault without the slightest interruption. Laughing and calling out to her familiar, the girl seems to be reveling in the gruesomeness, as the prickling pain becomes increasingly intense and blood runs down my arm.

"I must bite you, Anna," Dorothy continues, her voice gleeful. "It is my command. And so I must hurt you."

CHAPTER 3

For false christs and false prophets will arise and perform great signs and wonders, so as to lead astray.
—**Matthew 24:24**

Nathaniel Ingersoll's ordinary is not particularly lively this evening. There are only a few patrons here warming by the hearth. Perhaps the news of the afflictions is keeping them away. Nathaniel and my brother Edward have joined me at my table this evening, and our conversation seems more intense than usual.

"We mustn't be too hasty, Thomas," Nathaniel says. He can be too wise for his own good, and he is playing his part well tonight. He is undoubtably a good man, but his goodness can often prevent pragmatism. "We have to be cautious in how we pursue this business."

Nathaniel and Edward have been my firm allies for as long as I can remember. Both are deacons of the church, and the three of us enjoy a near-weekly communion at

Nathaniel's tavern. Although I will not deny that our discussions can sometimes devolve into the frivolous, particularly when we have had a drink or two, we mostly trade important news with one another or conduct business. On this night, however, we cannot help but discuss the matter that has transfixed this community for weeks.

"You can say that we should not rush to judgment," I say, "but you are forgetting that I saw the reverend's girls with my own eyes. I witnessed their wretched condition, and I can say with great authority that it was not of this world."

As soon as I finish speaking, Edward—ever my younger brother and friendly rival—inserts a rebuttal. "That is not for you to say. You know there could be any number of reasons for the girls' condition."

I am not about to let my brother get the last word. "Edward, I was in the room when Dr. Griggs informed Reverend Parris that the evil hand was upon them. I know that of which I speak."

"Ha! You, of all people, should not be trusting the word of Dr. Griggs," Edward retorts. "You must forget that you have made your feelings about this man quite clear to both of us."

Trying to refocus our attention on the matter at hand, I reply, taking a firm and direct approach, "Please understand—both of you—that it is not my wish for such events to be occurring here. I will concede that you both might eventually be proven correct in this matter, but as leaders in this community, gentlemen, it is our responsibility to be prepared, come what may."

My tone seems to accomplish its goal. A seriousness wafts over our table like a mist.

"We take your meaning, Thomas," Nathaniel says. "Tell us, how do you propose that we proceed?"

Upon asking his question, I can see Nathaniel's eyes shift toward my brother as if they have somehow been in concert on this matter. Yet both men's eyes quickly return to me in anticipation of my response.

"You may be surprised to learn that I have no answer," I say. "All I am suggesting is that we must be prepared with a plan should this matter turn into something we must address."

"You are correct," Edward says quickly. He seems to be encouraged by my lack of certainty. "We must be prepared for whatever may come."

"We should also be prepared to go about our lives as we always have," Nathaniel argues, his usual magnanimity shining through. "We should never condone any behavior that is not properly measured."

"Of course," I say with perhaps a bit too much exasperation in my voice. "Nobody is suggesting that we should engage in anything untoward. However, as a longstanding member of this community, you must recognize the ways in which we have slipped in our responsibilities."

Edward raises his eyebrows, clearly intrigued by my shifting line of reasoning. "By all means, my dear brother, enlighten us with your thoughts on this subject," he says.

His reply, I know, is intended as a taunt. I stare sharply at him. It feels as if I have been transported back to our days as children, when the two of us would regularly vie for our father's attention.

"Tell me, Edward," I ask him directly, "are we the city upon the hill that we have always intended to be? Have we become the shining beacon that our grandfather expected us to be when he came here six decades ago?"

"Judge not, that you be not judged," Edward says. "All communities change over time. There is nothing unusual about it. Our grandfather, or any man from his generation, could not have foreseen how we would need to adapt to our surroundings here. You cannot say that we are not upholding the promise of our forefathers simply because that promise of the past does not look as you expect it should today."

Seemingly fearing that our conversation might devolve into a squabble between siblings, Nathaniel says quickly, "Gentlemen, we gather in my ordinary with regularity because we see eye to eye on a great many things, and I do not see how this is different from any other matter."

Nathaniel always takes well to his role as our sage.

"All your brother and I are saying, Thomas," he continues, "is that it would be unwise for anyone to rush to any conclusions. You are an intelligent man and I dare say you agree with this assessment, do you not?"

Perhaps more grateful for Nathaniel's diplomatic efforts than I expected, I give him a sympathetic look. He does not wait for my answer to his question before continuing: "You are correct that we must be prepared for anything, but we must also be prepared for this business to be nothing at all. Rejoice in hope, be patient in tribulation, be constant in prayer," he says, concluding with a wink and a nod to both myself and Edward.

"You are a wise man," I say with a smile. "Of course, I agree with you. No sane man would not agree with such a sentiment."

Still, I am unwilling to allow this great sage to have the final word.

"But I can quote scripture too, Nathaniel," I say after a short pause. "And in all circumstances take up the shield of faith, with which you can extinguish all the flaming darts of the evil one."

The two of them look at each other, then return their eyes to me.

"We must be prepared, gentlemen," I continue in a firm voice. "For we know not what might be ahead of us."

I hear a sound like the crash of a falling tree or a loud crack of thunder. Whatever it is wakes me in a flash, and I find myself suddenly sitting upright in my bed. After a moment or two of quiet, I detect the slightest movement in the darkness, near my door. It is accompanied by the muffled noises of what sounds like shuffling, as if somebody or something is struggling to make its way in my direction.

Overcome with fear, I blink my eyes rapidly, hoping I am just experiencing the remnants of my slumber. Perhaps it is all just a dream. Suddenly, I am startled by the unmistakable sound of a woman's voice, piercing breathlessly through the quiet darkness:

"You are not safe, Ann."

My body immediately tenses at the sound of the voice, and I am engulfed in chills from head to toe. My eyes dart frantically around the room in search of whoever has spoken. A moment later, I hear the voice again.

"Why did you not listen to her?"

It is clearer now. Still breathless and weak, but more confident than before.

"Mother?" I utter the word so meekly that it barely escapes my mouth. Yet it is the first thing that comes to my mind. Perhaps my mother has wandered into my room. Perhaps she wishes to check on me. Yet there is no response to my weak query.

After a moment or two of quiet—a moment or two of hope that whatever this is has ended—a sudden explosion of movement bursts before my eyes. As if out of nowhere, I see the shape of a woman standing brightly before me.

Her eyes are like fire, red and raging. Her hair is stringy and gray and seemingly composed of worms or tiny snakes. One of her bony and sharp fingers pokes me squarely in the stomach, causing a sudden jab of pain with each thrust. I do not—cannot—push this being away from me. Instead, I hold my arms at my sides and endure a barrage of sharp stabs into my torso.

"Dorothy warned you, but you did not listen to her."

The voice seems to be growing more confident now.

"Why do you ignore my child, Ann? She is wise, much wiser than her years. She has been nursed on the devil's milk."

The woman's words are frightening, but I manage a meek response. "Who are you? What do you want from me?"

"I am here to have you sign the devil's book, Ann."

The being comes closer to me, and I can see that her eyes are softer now and that her hair appears to be normal.

"You know me as a beggar, and my life appears to be difficult to you, but that is merely my disguise. The devil takes very good care of me. He ensures that I have everything that I need. I am rich beyond imagination because I have committed my soul to him."

The woman seems eager to speak now. Her words are flowing like a waterfall from her mouth.

"Dorothy has tried to guide you in her way, but she is only a child, so I have come to you now. You must sign the devil's book, Ann. You must make a contract with the underworld—or else your path will not be so forgiving."

"Goodwife Good?"

I can see more clearly now, and it is as if I have been struck by a lightning bolt. I am suddenly aware that Sarah Good is standing before me. I do not know her well, but she and her husband are beggars who regularly rely on the charity of others for their well-being.

"Why are you here?" I ask in a shivering voice, drenched in fear.

"I am only here to help you, Ann." Her tone is kind. As if she is trying to reassure me. "I wish to provide you with a path toward everlasting glory. How could you not desire such a thing?"

Unable to contemplate how or why Sarah Good could be standing before me in her condition, touting the virtues of the underworld, I command her to leave me. "Leave me! Let me be or I will call my father!"

I attempt to use both of my hands to push Goodwife Good away from me, but my hands seem not to touch anything at all. The specter, however, is suddenly gone in a flash, leaving no trace in its wake.

As I regain my composure in the silence and darkness that has once again engulfed my room, I can make out what seems to be the faintest of whispers, as if it is the gentlest of breezes tickling my ear: "You will learn of his power, Ann."

CHAPTER 4

Such a prayer offered in faith will heal the sick, and the Lord will make you well.

—James 5:15

"Through this great communion of believers, we will harness the power of the Almighty to wash away this evil . . ."

It was Reverend Parris's idea to conduct a vigil and engage in fasting so that we might assist our afflicted girls in their recovery. The vigil is meant to provide our citizens with something they can do in service to these poor children, and the reverend is preaching in his most dynamic manner. Reverend Hale and other pastors as far away as Boston have joined us here as well.

In truth, there is little that we can do for the girls. Dr. Griggs has proved useless and now we are turning to prayer and fasting. What else is there? I know from our discussions that the reverend is quite concerned about the situation, uncertain about what the future may hold for his daughter and niece.

"Let us fast and pray so that our children of God may be restored to full health."

As Reverend Parris finishes his sermon, George Jacobs, a man of nearly eighty years, struggles to rise from his seat with the help of his walking sticks. He is raising his hand in the air to indicate his desire to speak, and all eyes turn toward him. Standing before us, Jacobs is tall, if a bit stooped with age, and his long white hair follows loosely down the back of his neck.

"Reverend, as a child of Christ, I thank you for your words of comfort and perseverance," he says, his voice stronger than one might expect from a man of his age. "But I would be remiss to allow this opportunity to pass without speaking my own mind on this matter."

Those who had not been paying attention suddenly become quiet, eager to take in what Jacobs is poised to say.

"I have been on this Earth, by the grace of God, for longer than most have, and I will say my peace plainly so as not to waste any of my neighbors' valuable time." Jacobs looks around the meetinghouse as if he is a member of parliament settling into a speech. "It is my firm belief, dear neighbors, that what many of us here seem to hold true in regard to the case of these so-called 'afflicted' girls, is likely not the truth at all."

At the sound of Jacobs's words, the gathering becomes suddenly animated. Several people immediately cry out in opposition. Jacobs, seemingly having anticipated such a reaction, is unmoved.

"God has blessed me with the wisdom of age, my good neighbors," he continues, "and this wisdom has enabled me to see what many others cannot. I implore you to see reason in this matter. You must understand that the devil, in all of his wickedness, might wish for us to believe that he has afflicted these girls through his minions, even if that is not the case."

The crowd is now loudly shouting at Jacobs, trying to drown out his words. Reverend Parris steps forward with much haste to quiet them down with a raised hand.

"Good people," the reverend says in his most boisterous voice, "please allow Goodman Jacobs to speak his peace. We may not agree with his assessment of our situation, but he has earned the right to have his say on this matter."

At this admonition, the gathering falls silent. Reverend Parris then gives Jacobs an uncomfortable glance with shifting eyes, seemingly signaling to him that he should continue.

"Thank you, Reverend Parris," Jacobs says, before turning back toward the audience and continuing. "My dear friends, I ask you to consider that the devil might wish for us to be set against one another. It might be the very outcome for which he has hoped. Because of this, we must tread lightly in our assumptions about things of which we do not know well."

The gathering erupts again in jeers, prompting Reverend Parris to step forward and usher Jacobs away. The optimism that the reverend's thoughtful preaching had generated has now been entirely soured. Many people take their leave entirely.

As he has done before, George Jacobs goes about his business with the surety and confidence of a wealthy man. For men like Jacobs, the truth will always be damned if it does not suit their needs. Despite his ill-mannered intrusion upon this sacred vigil, Jacobs shuffles away unscathed with his head held high. I ask, are these the actions of a community set on vengeance?

Mercy is always the first to rise each morning, starting the fire and tending to her duties before the others have awakened. She has served our home now for two months, coming here from the eastern frontier. Her sister lives in Salem and that is what brought her here. After Mother had baby Timothy last year, our family needed assistance, and Mercy has proven to be invaluable. I am grateful for what she does for me as well.

I have grown quite fond Mercy. At nineteen, she is seven years older than I am, but she does not treat me like a child.

Instead, she is a welcome respite from my daily drudgery. As the oldest daughter, I am obliged to care for my younger siblings, Ebenezer and Deliverance, who are but six and four years old. Thomas is just a year younger than I am and quite capable of managing his own affairs.

As I drag myself in a slumbrous haze past her quarters this morning, I see Mercy still lying upon her bed, seemingly fast asleep. I approach her to make sure that she is well and, as I do this, her eyes suddenly fly open, looking remarkably bright. It is as if she has been fully awake and waiting for me to pass by to reveal her alertness to me.

"Anna! Anna! He is after me!"

I cannot tell if Mercy is having a dream or if something else is troubling her.

"What is the matter, Mercy? What do you mean?"

"We must hide from him, Anna. He can't see us like this. Run, girl, run!"

I am unsure what is happening. Mercy appears to be fully awake, yet she seems to be engulfed in a nightmare. I hesitate for a moment before grabbing her shoulder and lightly shaking her. When I do so, Mercy immediately bolts upright in her bed. Her back is as straight as a board and her eyes stare vacantly forward.

"Mercy?" I ask tentatively. "Can you hear me?"

There is no response.

For a moment, I think about fetching my father but hesitate when I worry about what might result from his being witness to such a situation. Instead, I clap my hands heartily in front of Mercy's face in the hope that it might release her from her stupor. After three or four loud claps of my hands, Mercy falls back upon her bed limply, closing her eyes as if she is asleep. The tension in her face and body is entirely gone.

Once I can see that she is breathing normally, I gently put my hand on her cheek, hoping she might wake without starting. Slowly, she begins to stir, as if she is just waking up from a long winter's nap.

"Anna, dear," she says. "What are you doing here?"

"Are you all right, Mercy?" The urgency in my voice seems to startle her.

"Why, of course. Why would you ask such a thing?"

Incapable of explaining what I have witnessed, I choose not to say anything more. "You are behind your time, but do not worry. We will handle our chores together."

"You are too kind to me, Anna," Mercy says as her brightest smile lights up her face.

CHAPTER 5

The Lord said unto my Lord, sit thou at my right hand, until I make thine enemies thy footstool.
—**Acts: 2:34–35**

I can see it in her eyes. They are wild and filled with tension. They betray Sarah Osborne's unease to everyone who notices them. They reflect a deep and exhausting conflict that must be growing and building inside of her. I cannot help but stifle a merciful thought for her given her sorry state. Yet despite my forbearance, I am unable to ignore the scourge that she and the others have brought to our village—to my very home now. None of us can rightfully ignore such a thing. These three women, Osborne, Sarah Good, and Tituba, have all been accused and arrested and are to be questioned at Ingersoll's today. As I cast my sight upon the disheveled Osborne, I cannot ignore a growing revulsion at the thought of her pleas for mercy, which are surely soon to come.

I have just finished a drenching ride in the middle of a raging tempest, and when I open the door to Ingersoll's, dripping from the deluge, Osborne is the first person who comes into my focus. Hobbled and barely able to stand, the old woman is hunched and in chains before a crowd of men. The damp air is heavy and stifling, making it difficult to breathe.

This horror has spread to my own home now. Anna has told me about her visit from the specters of Sarah Good and her daughter, Dorothy. She says they have hurt her. It seems that the insidious nature of the devil can lead him to strike at the most pious among us, as well as the weakest and most excitable. My daughter is among the afflicted now, including Elizabeth and Abigail, Mary Walcott, Elizabeth Hubbard, and likely many others whom we are not even aware of yet. It is easy to see why the devil's victims are girls. Their weak and excitable constitutions make them easy targets for his cruel endeavors. I fear that this is only the beginning. Because of Anna's condition, my presence at these examinations is imperative.

My perilous journey here has left me feeling as if I am a character in the Bible—the Almighty testing the strength of my faith. Yet my safe passage through the tempest to Ingersoll's ordinary is a clear sign of God's mercy. I vowed during my journey that if I made it to this tavern where these examinations are taking place, if I did not fall from my horse in a soaking heap, maimed and shivering in the gloom, then it is God's will that my plan should be brought forth.

I want only to prevent our home from being eviscerated by those who would like to see us in harm's grasp. It seems inconceivable to me that we rub shoulders daily with those who wish to destroy us. We go about our lives, praying in the meetinghouse or working in our fields, with such wretches steady by our side, toiling busily to hasten our defeat and destroy all that is good. I will never understand their purpose, but these three accused women might represent the very tip of the arrow. Therefore, these proceedings cannot be taken lightly. I am pleased that the showing at Ingersoll's is strong, despite the storm. It would appear that many of us understand this threat.

Judge Hathorne is the magistrate presiding over the examinations. He sits upon his dais, pompous and fleshy, having ascended to his position purely as a result of his wealth. He owns land across this province and well beyond it. I cannot say that his considerable means have suitably prepared him for this duty. I pray that he is up to the task set before him.

Sarah Good is the first to be questioned. Her impoverishment and profane existence is well known to us. I had half expected her to ask me for a pine tree shilling when her eyes caught me at the tavern door. She has always been eager to take advantage of our Christian charity, taking full advantage of her innocent children to bilk the caring people of this community out of their earnings. Why should we expect anything different given her current circumstances? After her father drowned himself when she was but a girl, she became a lost soul: testing our magnanimity, cursing those who would not yield to her incessant entreaties for scraps of silver or food. Her stringy brown hair is matted to her forehead; her soiled clothing and the stench that regularly emanates from her unwashed body are intolerable. We should not have to bear such things in a civilized society.

"Why did you go away muttering from Reverend Parris's house?" Hathorne does not even bother to look up at Good as he mumbles his question. For a second or two, there is silence, a pregnant pause. It seems as if Good may be knocked off balance. Perhaps she is wondering who it was that saw her leaving the parsonage and reported it to the authorities.

"I did not mutter," she says finally. "I thanked him for what he gave my child."

Like so many of our God-fearing citizens, Reverend Parris had simply given in to Good's incessant begging and offered his ample Christian charity to this woman's wretched child. The reverend's selfless act has enabled Good to claim she was simply thanking him for his thoughtfulness rather than cursing him on behalf of the devil as she walked away from his home with a mutter upon her lips.

"Have you made no contract with the devil?"

It is the best Hathorne can muster under the circumstances, knowing full well the denial that will come from Good. Yet her denials of what we know to be true will not save her now. It has been an inauspicious beginning to these proceedings for Judge Hathorne, but even his poor showing in examining Sarah Good will not save her from her fate.

The men have become unsettled as a result of Good's questioning. Many are openly jeering at her as she is removed from the premises by the constable. I take some small solace in their discontent. I appreciate that I am not alone in my frustrations. Some have come here with a focused desire to preserve our God-fearing community. Our numbers are so great, in fact, that Ingersoll's ordinary, where such legal proceedings usually take place, can no longer contain us, and we are forced to move to the meetinghouse down the road to conduct the balance of our business. I am thankful that the rain has tapered into a drizzle as we make the short walk to the new venue.

Laboring to carefully navigate the muddy road, I feel a hand touch my shoulder. When I turn around, I am pleased to see Edward beside me. His face appears worn and tired. Hard lines are creasing his forehead, and a deep concern seems to be set into his eyes. Nonetheless, I am heartened by the sight of him.

"What do you make of the proceedings, Thomas? Do they meet your expectations?" He asks his question with a sly look in his eye, but I cannot tell if he is being sarcastic with me.

"It is too soon to know," is all I offer in return.

Edward is a deacon in the First Church of Danvers and, because of this, he is often privy to news that I am not, given the proclivity of whisperings among the clergy.

"When I learned that the marshals had collected the women, I was eager to be present at their examinations. Of course, I knew that I would see you here, too, Thomas."

I am pleased to see his eyes come to life as he speaks. Edward's eyes always twinkle when he is thinking.

Once we assemble inside the meetinghouse, it is Sarah Osborne's turn to be questioned, and she wastes little time in revealing her nefarious interactions.

"I was frightened in my sleep by a thing like an Indian." Osborne's voice seems to be shaking with fear, making it difficult to understand her. "It was all black and it pricked me in my neck and pulled me around the house by my head."

Osborne's strange revelation is like a bolt of lightning, transforming the room in a flash. Soon, every eye has shifted to Hathorne, seated at his hastily constructed bench, hovering just above the rest of us in the meetinghouse. He seems to be the only person who has not been affected by Osborne's unusual recollections.

"Did you see anything else?" Hathorne's meek question seems to deflate the room.

"No," is all Osborne says in response, visibly relieved to leave this line of questioning behind.

Hathorne is content to move on with his rote questioning. He appears eager to be done with this matter altogether. I hold my tongue, barely, but I can tell that Hathorne's feebleness is inducing a sharp reaction from many of the others in attendance. One man—I cannot see who he is from my vantage point in the crowded room—shouts something to the effect of "We must know more!" and his shaming words seem to shake Hathorne out of his stupor and compel him to action.

"Hath the devil ever deceived you?" Hathorne asks, more urgently now.

"I do not know the devil," Osborne replies. "I have never seen him."

Hathorne is either unwilling or unable to press Osborne any further, and a murmur builds in the room once more. A few of the men even leave entirely, presumably disgusted that the examination is not yielding what they expected.

I cannot understand Hathorne. Why is he choosing not to inquire further about this strange dark being? He is not examining some petty thief. This is something far more sinister, and he must be steadfast in his duties. For all we know, Osborne's black man is Satan himself. We cannot dismiss such a thing so easily.

"I was more likely to be bewitched than to be a witch," Osborne utters indignantly as Hathorne finishes questioning her. She is fully in control of her emotions now and wears an indelicate look of pride upon her face, seemingly pleased to have gotten the best of this man. Yet her denials betray what we can so plainly see: The devil has her in his grasp. It is he who appears to be in control now. Hathorne may have been duped with ease by her antics, but not all of us will be caught unawares. Osborne has scandalized this village for far too long, marrying her servant and stealing land that rightfully belonged to her neighbors. Has she accomplished these ignoble deeds in partnership with the underworld? Has the devil now fully completed his triumph over her? The storm that I had witnessed in Osborne's eyes earlier seems to have resolved itself now. She sits smugly before us, apparently at peace with her surroundings.

Now it is the heathen slave Tituba's turn before Hathorne. She is wearing her diminutive smile, perhaps unaware of the trouble she is facing. Or perhaps she is a bit more clever than she ought to be, despite her feeble attempts to pretend otherwise. She does not fool me with this show of hers, even if others are more easily taken in by it.

Tituba listens intently, concentrating hard in order to understand Hathorne's dull queries. The gathered men seem to be accepting the reflective denials of these women now, and it is lulling us all into a complacent stupor.

"The devil came to me and bid me to serve him," Tituba says.

There is an audible gasp in the room at her admission. It is a jolt that awakens us all from our slumber.

When Reverend Parris first arrived in Salem, I warned him that Tituba's presence might disquiet our community in ways he was not prepared for, that her fraternization with the women and children here might be a corrupting force upon them. However, I should not hold the reverend at fault for Tituba's transgressions. He is a worldly man—born in London and having lived in Barbados where he acquired Tituba. He should be admired for his experiences, not scorned for them. Yet the workings of a New England village are quite different from those of a hedonistic island in the West Indies. The reverend was, perhaps, a bit too ignorant of this reality before he arrived here, too sanguine about the goodness of those around him to fret about such matters. He has learned his lesson now, as we all must do from time to time. Tituba is no doubt of great value to Reverend Parris, but her dusky exoticism has proven too alluring for some here, especially for our children, who desire to fraternize with her often. Tituba plays along in her coquettish manner. It is unbecoming. She claims innocence and acceptance of our ways, but might she be making a mockery of our charity?

"He showed me a little yellow bird," she says, "and he told me that tomorrow he would show me more beautiful things and that he would let me keep the pretty yellow bird for myself."

As she speaks, Tituba has a child-like gleam in her eye and that ever-present smile upon her face. It seems as if she is coveting the devil's gifts. He has offered her all the beauty of this world in return for her devotion to him. Yet perhaps it is Tituba's own devotion to Reverend Parris that has compelled her to tell the truth now, before the magistrate. Perhaps the reverend is correct about her after all. Whatever the case, her testimony has presented us with an opportunity.

My plan first struck me, fully formed, the day I saw Elizabeth sprawled upon the floor of the parsonage some weeks back. It was like a lightning bolt sent from Zeus. The others who are attending these examinations are likely driven by the desire for justice. As they rode through the storm, it was raw emotion that kept them on their mounts, clutching their reins with as much fortitude as they could muster. They wish to ensure that these crimes are avenged. It is honorable, and I commend each of them for their pure judgment. Yet my own desires are driven by something shrewder. To be sure, I, too, seek justice. My disdain for witchcraft is unrelenting, as it should be. However, the justice I seek transcends the feral and base desires of my comrades. My aims are higher-minded.

Salem is in a far inferior state now than it was during the days of our fathers. I am at pains to say this, but there can be no argument about this fact. Perhaps it is typical of any growing community, but we must first accept this reality or else we will be powerless to improve upon it. Like any good leader, I want to believe that my efforts to carefully usher Salem along the path God has chosen for us should be one victory after the next. Alas, as any leader worth his salt recognizes, such business is not so easy.

Despite my pessimism about our current situation, I will admit that most of my neighbors are sitting comfortably at the right hand of the Father. They are here in this meetinghouse to do the work required of them to ensure that we remain fixed upon a virtuous path. Yet the fact remains that their noble efforts and countless acts of selflessness have not improved our situation. We are threatened on all sides now. We are still without a charter from the Crown; the natives ominously surround us and are spoiling for a fight; and the devil and his followers are seemingly nipping at our heels, scheming to undermine us at every turn. Each of these dangers works against our glory, attempting to tear us apart like a wolf would a sheep.

The Almighty approves of our attempts to seek His grace and mercy. I believe that is why God has inspired my plan and spared me on my treacherous journey to these examinations. I must do my part to serve our community, as I always have, as my father and grandfather did before me. It is a grave and important responsibility, and regardless of the challenges that it presents, we all have our orders. We must not abdicate our responsibility and rebuke the tasks God has set before us. Like my father and namesake, I have vowed to do my duty regardless of what it may cost. The Putnam name will not be tarnished by my negligence and inaction at such a time of need.

Is our village still a model of Christian charity? Do we remain a City upon a Hill? Some pretend that it is so, while others are afraid even to ask such questions at all. No leader of men can willingly believe untruths or cowardly dodge what he is required to face. These questions must be asked and answered with honesty, whether the answers are suitable or not. Is our beloved Salem to be handed over to the devil? Have we become just another heedless village in this land, dizzied by the meandering and hopeless pursuit of enlightenment while becoming entangled in a morass of avarice and vice?

I refuse to believe that is the path God intends for us. He is testing our mettle. He is asking us to choose between good and evil. He has left it up to us to choose our course, as He always does. These questions must be asked, and leaders must be prepared with answers and strong actions.

This dark moment on the cusp of a new century might foretell a new dawn that we cannot yet see. Is it not always darkest before dawn?

I can hear Marley, my father's horse, neighing and snorting in the distance, and I am grateful that they will be home soon. I am eager to learn about the examinations of the women. I am less anxious than I have been in recent days and am feeling better today than usual, thank God. As my father slowly makes his way home through the soggy mud, I am grateful not to be adding to his burdens with more news about my affliction.

It is not his usual manner, but Father seems uncomfortable, almost frightened, of me in recent days. He has not looked at me directly since witnessing Betty and Abby's afflictions at the parsonage. He seems to have been moved greatly by that experience. When Father opens the door and sees me standing before him, he quickly shifts his eyes away without a word.

Is it fear or shame he is feeling toward me?

Mother's health has been fragile for many years now. She has good days still, but when she is not feeling well, Father often speaks to me, his oldest child, in her stead. He shares his concerns in a way that makes me feel closer to him. He does not protect me as other fathers often protect their daughters. I am grateful for that, but the news I have shared about my affliction—or whatever it is that has been affecting me—seems to have changed him in some way.

"I am sorry, Father."

It is all I can think to say to him after he pours himself a drink and takes a seat in his chair by the hearth, his eyes still avoiding me. I hope my words will spur him into his usual existence with me. I would do anything to bring my father back to me.

"There is no need for apologies, child," he says with a sigh, his voice quiet and morose. At last, he looks in my direction.

"Whatever I have done to bring this on—"

"Stop, Anna. There is no need." My father says this with a raised hand of exasperation as he looks at me with a tired glance, though one that is not without compassion.

"You mustn't speak of apologies, Anna," he says. "The devil is cunning, and if your condition is what we believe it to be, you have no reason for shame. You are to be pitied."

"Thank you, Father."

"I cannot stop my mind," my father says to me, seemingly content enough to speak to me once more. I have heard this phrase from him many times before. He often uses it as a means to spark a conversation.

"What do you mean, Father?" I wish nothing more than to encourage him.

"During the examinations, Tituba claimed that the devil urged her to sever their heads—the very girls that she is charged with caring for. What if she had done what the devil had commanded? She could have done so easily when nobody was around. How can there be such evil in our midst?"

Father speaks with a growing agitation as I listen to him intently.

"Tituba spoke so calmly about these things. She spoke of sailing through the air on a stick to do the devil's bidding. It was madness!" Running his hand through his hair in frustration, Father seems to recognize that he is losing control and attempts to collect himself with a deep breath. "I could only think of you, Anna. While Tituba spoke of these awful things, I could only think about what you must be enduring, my daughter . . ." He seems to want to say more, but instead he trails off and takes a long sip from his drink.

"I have been better lately, Father," I say, hoping to reassure him with my news. "It has been a few days now." I do not know how to refer to what is happening to me, so I often do not name it at all.

Father is not buoyed by this news as much as I had expected. He offers little more than a weak smile, and is clearly still lost in his own thoughts.

"Have you heard any news of Abby and Betty, Father?" I hope to use my question as a means of redirecting his thinking.

"Nothing."

Father's revelation about Tituba makes me think. I cannot help but wonder what the devil might compel me to do. Will he ask me to harm those who I love? I want to ask my father what he thinks about such things but I fear bringing it up to him while he is in this condition.

When I first learned about Betty and Abby's afflictions, I thought it was nothing more than their usual dramatics, just another ploy for them to gain the attention they both so desperately crave. Being in the parsonage, they get far more attention than the rest of us do, but I suppose the more attention one receives, the more one desires. Yet surely their condition cannot only be solely the result of their melodramatic nature.

Has Tituba done this?

It is another question I would like to ask Father. Tituba is nothing like the rest of us; she is full of contradictions: a slave, as the Lord has intended her to be, but also benevolent and God-fearing. She is a child in a woman's body, but her lusty beauty cannot easily be cast aside. There are many who do not like that she is here, but it is difficult to deny her goodness, nonetheless. She is kind, and she is especially fond of Betty. Tituba provides a mother's love to her. Could she be capable of the depravity of which Father speaks?

I have never witnessed an inkling of wickedness in Tituba's manner, at least not that I can remember. She often wishes me a good day in her broken language, her dark hair, in curls, mounted atop her head and a warm smile on her pretty face. She always seems to have a quick step. It is as if she is particularly eager to get to where she is going. I see her at the meetinghouse nearly every week. It seems to me that her devotion is most genuine. Of course, there is much we do not know about Tituba and her ways. Might she have brought this evil to us, even if she did so unwittingly? I pluck up my nerve to ask Father.

"Do you believe it is Tituba who has brought the evil hand upon us, Father?"

He sighs. "It would be difficult to believe she is faultless, but I am afraid the answer to your question is difficult for us to know."

Father's calm and contemplative manner encourages me to speak more.

"Perhaps she never had a chance against the devil's sorcery," I say. "No matter how devout she believes she is, perhaps the devil always had his heart set on Tituba in order to get to us."

I am impressed with my line of reasoning and eager to hear my father's response, but he merely says "Perhaps," before becoming lost in his own thoughts once again. Still, I persevere.

"Perhaps it will all simply go away. Perhaps, soon, we will not have to think of these things again." I say this with *more than a little hope in my voice, believing my optimism might break through to him. Yet he offers no response at all. Instead, Father stares silently into some unknowable abyss as he raises his nearly empty glass to his lips.*

CHAPTER 6

But the Lord is faithful. He will establish you and guard you against the evil one.

—2 Thessalonians 3:3

It is the sound of a rabid animal: a low, screeching growl that seems entirely barbaric in its origins. It is not very loud, yet it appears that we both can clearly hear it as we sit warming by the hearth. I am hoping—perhaps with more than a little desperation—that this strange noise is somehow emanating from outside of our home; perhaps it is a nearby fox or a wolf that has made its way just outside our door.

Not wanting to create any undue commotion, I cast a careful, uneasy glance toward our visitor, Reverend Lawson, hoping I might be able to gauge his level of concern and perhaps encourage his discretion. Both of us avert our eyes as soon as they meet, seemingly too embarrassed to pursue the matter further. I am relieved he has not said anything. Still, the look upon his face is worrying and he is shifting uncomfortably in his seat, perhaps thinking about how he might take his leave. The reverend's tea sits untouched on the table before him. Having only spent a quarter of an hour together, it seems politeness is preventing his hasty exit from our home.

I had been pleased to see Reverend Lawson in the village this morning and I eagerly asked him to visit before setting off for his journey back to Boston. He is a fine pastor, even if he never had the opportunity to find success in Salem. He left us after four years, but he did his duty well. I believe he has always viewed me as a keen ally, and I was pleased when he gratefully accepted my invitation. It was not long, however, before I realized that today is not a good day for my wife. Visitors in our home can make the situation more difficult for her. Not wanting to put Reverend Lawson off, I hoped for the best. Ann still has moments when she is nearly as lucid as she was in our early days together, even if those moments are fewer now than they once were. I suppose I thought the reverend might ignite some spark within her from the past, given her fondness for him. Perhaps it was too much for me to expect such things. From the moment he stepped foot in our home, the reverend has been most disquieted.

The rocking chair has been in our family for decades. My father carefully crafted it himself and built it to last for generations, the way furniture was built in his day, with an attention to craftsmanship that seems lost to us now. It is a fine piece that stands out as one of our most prized possessions. It rests in a place of honor by the hearth. We do not sit in the chair often for fear that we might wear it out or damage it in some way. It was my mother's favorite, and as I look upon it now, bathing in the reflected glow of the fire, I find myself awash in warm feelings. Perhaps it is odd that a piece of furniture can induce such emotion in a man, but I cannot deny its power over me.

"Get away from me now!"

My wife is suddenly shouting at the top of her lungs as she stares menacingly toward my mother's rocking chair, repeating it over and over again in quick succession with a wild and determined look upon her face: Get away from me now, get away from me now, get away from me now.

"Ann!" I interject as expediently as I can. "What is the matter?"

My wife's focus remains firmly upon the empty rocking chair. Her eyes are passionately fixed upon it.

The chair appears to be entirely vacant and still. As I glance at Reverend Lawson, his perplexed and uncomfortable countenance betrays his own confusion over the matter.

"That evil woman!" Ann shouts. "Get her out of my house!"

As my wife continues shouting, I attempt to calm her and notice that Reverend Lawson has placed his hands tightly over his ears and is wearing an uncomfortable grimace upon his face.

"I am afraid she is much overworked and tired, reverend."

He gives me only a pained look in response.

After several more frightful and confusing moments, my daughter appears in the room. At first, she does not seem to be speaking words at all, but instead is uttering some manner of indistinguishable foreign tongue made up only of odd and twisted syllables rather than fully formed and recognizable words. The grotesque sounds spill out of her mouth in an unusual cadence, with sounds running into one another in a jumble. After what seems like several seconds of this, Anna eventually makes herself clear.

"It is Goodwife Nurse," she says to us. "She is sitting in grandmother's chair. She is laughing heartily at us."

"What are you saying, Anna?" I ask in response to her nonsensical explanation. "Tell us what you mean! I see nothing in that chair!"

The reverend rises to his feet and begins backing slowly toward the door, as if he is trying to take his leave from a bloody murder scene.

"I see her, too, Father," Anna says calmly. "It seems that I can see what Mother sees."

Anna's words—spoken through the continued din of my wife's hysterics—hit me like a strong gale.

"Rebecca Nurse is rocking in Grandmother's chair," my daughter continues. "She is enjoying herself, Father, reveling in our distress."

"Are you trying to embarrass me in front of Reverend Lawson?" I ask.

My daughter shakes her head. Soon, tears begin to stream down Anna's cheeks as she tries to comfort her mother, who is now crouched down by the hearth, seemingly trying to escape Goody Nurse's ridicule by climbing up the chimney.

"You are safe, Mother. You are safe. Nobody will harm you here." Anna is doing her best to calm her mother through her own tears and concern.

"I am sorry, Thomas," Reverend Lawson says in a dull whisper, as if he is barely able to get the words out of his mouth. "I have a long journey ahead of me."

In truth, I had forgotten about Reverend Lawson's presence entirely. As he retrieves his coat and hat and quickly moves for the door, I cannot help but wonder what he is thinking and what he might tell others about what he has seen here. I start to speak to him but hesitate. I am lost for words. It seems that concerns about discretion are of little importance now.

Does he see me sitting here in the meetinghouse?

Reverend Parris must see me. I am where I always am during meetings. I am exactly where I have been when he has seen me before. He must be aware of me now.

I am listening more attentively to him than I ever have before, though it is much more difficult for me now, given the torturous thoughts swimming around inside my consciousness.

Does he know? Does he think badly of me? As he scans the congregation while he preaches, what will he think of me when I catch his eye?

Am I just another sinner to him now? Perhaps I am responsible for bringing this shame upon us. Maybe I have poisoned our glory with my ignominy?

". . . Dreadful witchcraft broke out here a few weeks ago," Reverend Parris says, his cadence firm and certain. There is anger in his voice as well as strength. Or is that disappointment I hear? No matter. He will never shy away from a fight.

"One of you is the devil." He repeats this phrase again and again during his sermon. "One of you is the devil. . . ."

Is it me? Am I Reverend Parris's Judas?

My mind is racing like a raging river in springtime. Obscure thoughts from its darkest recesses are being dislodged and come forward in a flurry to haunt me day and night. Despite my disordered mind, I am trying my best now to listen to the Reverend's words, to hide my wretched torment from him. Can he see that I have allowed the devil to deceive me?

"There are such devils in the church..."

His words are becoming more urgent. Does he know I am the devil? I have always been aware that I have faults. I know I must have brought this upon myself. I have allowed myself to fall into some devious trap set by the devil. Reverend Parris has made it clear that those of us who do not live purely by the Scriptures as the Lord has intended for us will sink our cherished community, as a heavy anchor would a tiny vessel. The reverend has told us we are all capable of the most devious depravity. We are all susceptible to the vilest temptations. Has the devil saved the worst of his depravity for me?

"Christ knows how many of these devils there are in his churches..."

The reverend seems to be relishing his words now. He is saying them with a half-smile set upon his face and an almost imperceptible nodding of his head. He is reveling in the glory of God's omnipotence.

"You see, here was a true church, sincere converts, and sound believers; and yet here was a devil among them..."

He is angry. Angry at us, displeased that the devil has found his way into his own church. I suppose I have been duped, despite my steadfastness. Perhaps I have not lived by the Word of God closely enough. Perhaps I have allowed the devil in his cleverness to deceive me through his unscrupulous servants who lurk in the dark.

I hope I might receive some comfort for my pain, even if I do not deserve it. I know I have been a disappointment—to God, to Reverend Parris—but now I wish for nothing more than some reassurance that I am not alone. I have been ignorant of the ways of the underworld; I cannot deny this. I have been too welcoming of its deviousness. I am the only one to blame for my own torment; I know this to be true.

The reverend should use me as an example for everyone, a useful illustration of how a person must be mindful of the scheming that is constantly swirling around. Yet once he has done so, once he has made me his example for all to heed, I beg him to show mercy upon me. I need grace now more than I ever have before.

"We are either saints or devils: The Scripture gives us no medium..."

His words are animated by strength and energy. He is a truth-teller. He speaks to us in ways that the pastors before him never did. He is a sturdy and powerful man, both in body and mind. He is never afraid to say what we need to hear to live a life that is closer to what God intends for us. His language is firm and muscular, compelling us to pay close attention to him. Even those who are not interested are unable to turn away from it.

The other pastors were cautious and hesitant, but Reverend Parris is sure of himself and confident in his knowledge of the Word. The others were more likely to tell us what we wanted to hear—that we are God's chosen people, that we are living out His plan with perfection—even if it was untrue. It is always easier to ignore our many shortcomings. Their desire for our love and admiration overpowered their desire to tell the truth.

Salem is a difficult place for pastors. So many of them have not had the courage required for such a position. They took the path of least resistance. Reverend Parris is not like the others. He is not afraid to shout the truths that must be told at the top of his voice. He is warning us against the devil, but are we listening to him? Do we hear his teachings? I pray we can harness God's power and fight with a determined zeal, just as he is saying we must.

"There are certain sins that make us devils . . ."

Am I a devil now?

CHAPTER 7

The Lord knows I have not hurt them. I am an innocent person.

—Rebecca Nurse

"What do you say, child? Has this woman hurt you?"

As he utters the words *this woman*, Hathorne points a harsh finger in the direction of Rebecca Nurse and glares unsympathetically at Abigail Williams, whom he is questioning. The magistrate seems ablaze today, perhaps more cognizant of the role he is playing in these important affairs now. He certainly must notice Reverend Parris steadfastly recording what is transpiring before us.

"Yes, she beat me this morning." Despite her affliction, Abigail answers Judge Hathorne's query with a studied calmness and the slightest hint of pride.

As the magistrate turns his attention to Anna, however, she does not show similar restraint. My daughter is only capable of mustering a brief nod of her head in response to

Hathorne's question before dissolving into a grievous fit, wailing and crawling upon the floor of the meetinghouse as she pounds her fists and feet hard into the floorboards.

"We need order! Please restrain this child!" Hathorne bellows his commands to nobody in particular, and I move quickly toward Anna to comfort her as best I can. I cannot deny, however, that I am shaken by her display: wild and full of rage. My wife, who is with us at the examination as well, makes no attempt to comfort her grieving daughter, remaining quietly seated and staring straight ahead, unmoved by the chaos erupting around her.

Once order is restored, Hathorne turns his attention to the accused. "Goodwife Nurse, what do you say to these accusations against you?"

"I can say before my Eternal Father I am innocent and God will clear my innocency."

As Hathorne continues his questioning, Rebecca Nurse remains steadfast in her denials. She claims to be nothing more than a God-fearing woman of age, but I know what she is capable of. There are far too many here who will never regard this old woman as anything but a pious and righteous being. They are as sure of her innocence as I am of her devilishness. Such divisiveness seems to be the way of our world now.

"Are you an innocent person relating to this witchcraft?"

As Hathorne attempts to gain a confession from Goody Nurse, my wife is suddenly charged with vigor. Rising from her seat like a phoenix, she screams at Goody Nurse.

"Did you not bring the Black Man with you? Did you not tempt me, you old hag!"

Ann's words rush out of her in a merciless growl. She seems incapable of keeping them inside.

"Do you not see what you are doing?" she goes on. "When you move your hands, these girls are afflicted. You stand there with dry eyes when these eyes are wet." At my wife's reference to wet eyes, she gestures to Anna and Abigail, causing a tangle of accusations and denials that amount to a cacophony of indistinguishable noise.

"The Lord knows I have not hurt them," Nurse responds, using her most robust voice in a nearly impossible attempt to rise above the growing din. "I am an innocent person. You do not know my heart!"

It takes ten minutes or more before Judge Hathorne and his assistant can settle the meetinghouse down. Despite Hathorne's spirited attempts to press Goodwife Nurse for a confession, she holds fast in her denials. Our progress seems to have stalled. It seems Hathorne's best efforts have fallen short.

"They are saying that the Black Man is whispering in your ear," Hathorne says, gesturing to the afflicted girls, "that there are birds about you as we are speaking. What do you say to this, Goodwife Nurse?"

"It is all false. I am clear."

Despite her coolness in response, every movement of Nurse's head or hand during her questioning seems to create a requisite response of agony from Anna, Abigail, and my wife. As Nurse's hands move, sharp cries of pain come forth from all three.

"Do you believe these afflicted persons are bewitched?" Hathorne asks.

"I do think they are."

So, Goody Nurse does not deny that they are afflicted, yet she does not take responsibility for it. It seems Hathorne has been beaten again. Nurse is like an unmovable wall, unwilling to give an inch. Yet the final question, seemingly produced with little thought and with the expectation of the usual response, provides Hathorne with a breakthrough.

"What do you think of this?" he asks Goody Nurse with a shrug of his shoulders and a look toward the afflicted girls.

"I cannot help it," Nurse says, "if the devil may appear in my shape."

During the moments when my affliction overtakes me, I want to disappear. I want to evaporate into the air like a fine mist.

I frantically race about the room, looking to tuck myself into some cupboard or dark corner like a cat about to birth a litter of kittens. I attempt to twist my limbs around me in a comforting cocoon, but there is no comfort to be found. I want nothing more than to reduce myself to an insignificant speck of dust and be blown away into oblivion.

Oh, I would do anything to take away the incessant ache that hovers over me and then blows through me suddenly like a storm gale rushing between the branches of a tree. This darkness stalks me like a wolf waiting patiently for its prey. My skin is on fire. It burns without the least bit of relief. I scratch at my arms and legs violently, knowing it will make my condition worse but unaware of anything else that might relieve my suffering. If I could bury myself in some deep hole or fly away to the heavens to remove myself from this earth, I would do so in an instant. I would do anything to make this pain go away. I would give anything to save my family from the endless shame that my sinfulness has brought to their doorstep.

I do not know when he first appeared. It seems as if he has always been with me, but I know that cannot be the case. It cannot have been long ago, yet I have no memory of when I first laid my eyes upon him. He is entirely black from head to toe, all except for his eyes and his teeth, which he tries hard to hide from me. It is as if every inch of his body has been charred by some great inferno. Is it painful for him? Perhaps the pain is his reason for haunting me.

The contrast between his midnight skin and the brightness of his eyes is almost too much to bear. Yet I cannot seem to look away from him. He has transfixed me. I suppose that is what he wishes to do the most. He moves his dark body in ways I have not seen before. Is it meant to shock me? Is this how the devil goes about his business?

At first, his movements seemed random to me. He was like any man going about his business. I know now that nothing he does is by chance. Everything—even the slightest of his movements—is perfectly calculated to cause me distress and discomfort. He is clever; I cannot deny that fact. And he knows that he is clever. He has not spoken to me, but it is not necessary for him to speak in order to frighten me.

Can I not simply close my eyes and wish him away? Have I somehow asked him to haunt me? Is that why he is always by my side? Have I summoned him before me with my dark thoughts and deeds? I am compelled to watch the Black Man's every movement, even if it is the last thing that I would ever wish to do. As he moves, I cannot look away.

CHAPTER 8

SEPTEMBER 1675

DEERFIELD, MASSACHUSETTS

Seventeen years earlier

I am determined not to live until I have no country.
—**Metacom, leader of the Wampanoag**

"We are prepared for battle, gentlemen. This is our moment to be soldiers for God...."

Captain Lathrop's words are still ringing in my ears as I crouch, uncomfortable, against a large tree stump, many hours after hearing them in the early morning mist. I am alone now, lost in the fog of battle. The fighting today at Muddy Brook has been brutal. Even so, the captain's words have kept me company. What he told us was not unusual—he repeats the same sentiments often. It is his plain speaking that gives his words their power when he tells us, "We should never have believed we could live alongside such people. It was the so-called wisdom of our forefathers that has brought us to this point. We know, gentlemen, what the native is capable of. You and I have seen his depravity with our own eyes now. We know the evil that lurks inside of him. We know what darkness is within his deprived consciousness..."

The captain arrived in Salem from England, but it was not long before he had moved on elsewhere. I am certain he was put in charge of us because he was once an Essex man like we are, even if it was only for a moment. In a way, Captain Lathrop seems not to be from anywhere at all, and he does not pretend to be one of us.

Like the rest of us, Captain Lathrop is only trying to survive now. We are all the same, regardless of rank: simple, grizzled warriors trying to make it through another day. When the captain takes his whiskey, his anger bubbles up like a cauldron of boiling water. War makes men angry, and after many months of fighting, Captain Lathrop should be forgiven for his disposition, as should we all. He is prone to blasphemy and hard drinking, yet I believe God will forgive him for his transgressions.

The captain's words return to me: "Their time for grace has long since passed, gentlemen. We should have learned this lesson years ago, but we know it now, nonetheless. We have seen the native in his most depraved state. And it is a sight to which no God-fearing person should ever be witness...."

A fire burns inside the captain. I suppose it is burning within all of us now, ignited by this heinous conflict. It has been more barbaric than any of us could have expected it to be. Perhaps that is the lesson we have learned here. We should have foreseen how fiercely the natives would fight when faced with their imminent destruction. Their cruelty is appalling. Men are hacked to death, limbs removed like worthless tree branches; such unimaginable depravity cannot be understood by those who have not borne witness to it. We should have known there would be no glory in this war for anyone.

I shudder to think that God has been witness to what I have seen in these fields and forests and villages. There have been many moments these past two years when the men have desired to abandon this fight altogether and go back to living their simple lives as they did before, to never think about the natives again.

"Their day of reckoning has come," the captain has told us. "We are striking back at them with the full fury with which God has graced us. You, my soldiers, are doing God's work. We are changing the course of history with the power that has been anointed to us by the Almighty...."

Captain Lathrop's musings continue to come to me during the darkest of nights in the forest, when I am shivering in the cold and I startle at every crack of a tree branch or call of an insect. His words weave themselves within my mind. They have sustained me through the harshness of this war.

We have been skirmishing throughout the afternoon and I have now lost my line. I must have traveled several miles over the course of the day's fighting. My ammunition is spent. I am entirely separated from my comrades.

The sky is hazy, and the air is thick with heat and smoke. Despite it being the middle of the afternoon, it feels as if the sun has not completely risen in the sky. It seems as if I am living in some strange, perpetual twilight. I have not had much to eat or drink for days. My mouth is parched, and my eyes burn from the heat and smoke. I have been weakened by hunger, but I am used to such conditions now. I know I will eat soon enough. Still, it has become nearly impossible for me to gather my thoughts in such a state. The captain's words haunt me more than usual. My mind seems to be a reflection of the murkiness of the world around me.

I am trying my best to rest and steel myself before setting off on the journey back to where I think my men are located. It is unusually hot today, despite the waning summer. I do not mind the heat or being alone. Sometimes, I prefer being on my own, away from the noise and the banter of the other men. I am not afraid anymore, at least not as much as I was in the beginning. These past months have strengthened my resolve to survive.

As I sit against this tree stump, battling the murkiness inside my head, I catch sight of a native. He is perhaps no more than thirty yards away from me, leaning against a massive oak tree. It seems as if he is a dream, at first, some nightmare conjured up within my addled mind. I am sure he is as startled by the sight of me as I am by him, but he shows no fear on his face at all. Instead, he looks serene as he stares straight back at me with a piercing, steady glance. It is almost as if he sees through me. His cheeks and forehead are painted in an orange-red hue, and his long hair is a single shock of black on the top of his head. He is a warrior, adorned with strange paint on his bare chest.

I dare not shift my eyes away from him. I have made no movements, but I watch closely as he begins to slowly contort his mouth in some vulgar fashion, perhaps preparing to make a distress call to his comrades. I struggle to gather my wits as my mind races wildly. I labor to cut through the mist that has been clouding my judgment. I know I need to act quickly, but I am at a loss as to how to proceed. There is little doubt that his fellow warriors will be upon me soon. If I fail to make haste, I will soon be outnumbered and destined to meet my end in some undignified and gruesome manner.

My mind is ablaze as I search desperately for a response to my circumstances.

I should not expect to find a shred of mercy in this monster, and I will not reduce myself to a beggar, pleading for my life before a savage who will not care in the least about my fate. I know my only recourse is to respond as a vicious animal backed into a corner would do. My only option is to take on this warrior directly. I must fight him like a man who has everything to lose. I know he will not be expecting such valor from me.

As I take hold of my dagger and charge at the warrior in one swift motion, his startled reaction emboldens me. He seems to be frozen in place, unable to respond to my movement until I have already begun to swing my blade in a sweeping motion toward his chest. He catches my arm just before the blade penetrates his skin. Grappling upright for a few seconds, we both fall hard to the ground and continue our struggle on the forest floor. Each of us is grasping uncontrollably at the other, like wild animals fighting for our very existence. Digging our fingernails into skin and groping like mad men in the dirt, each of us is desperately trying to seize anything we can grasp to gain the upper hand.

There is no time to pray under such conditions, of course, but God, in his ever-present mercy, provides me with the strength I need to take full advantage of this heathen.

I feel a renewal of energy surging through my body—a clear moment of divinely inspired power—and, seizing the opportunity, I roll on top of the native and let out a wild and satisfying yelp as I feel the balance of power shift in my favor.

As we continue to grapple, the warrior maneuvers directly over a jagged stone laying harmlessly upon the ground and it wrenches painfully into his bare lower back. His sharp cries of agony betray what is happening to him, and I realize immediately what I must do. With a swift jab of my right arm, I plunge my dagger deep into the side of the warrior's neck.

The knife penetrates his skin more easily than I expected, and the results are far more bloody than I could have imagined. The warrior is bleeding profusely, gasping, and wheezing wildly. His eyes, when they were able to focus, take on a pleading expression. There is a look of sheer terror upon his bloodied face. It is like nothing I have ever witnessed before. It is the look of a man facing only fear and darkness ahead of him. It is the look of a man who is not awaiting God's mercy in the Kingdom of Heaven. In his attempts to staunch the profuse bleeding from his neck, the warrior's hands have smeared the paint from his chest onto his face. He looks disheveled and weak now.

God has seen to my safety. The warrior's comrades are nowhere to be found. The noises of his death throes, thankfully, fall only upon my own ears. As my strength begins to be restored, I feel a strong compulsion to witness this heathen's demise and descent into hell. I am not a dishonorable man, but I cannot say why I feel so compelled to watch him die. As he expires before me, I am overcome with feelings of peace and serenity. It is as if I am being commanded by the Almighty to act as His earthly witness, and I am doing as I have been told.

The warrior's pleading eyes have dulled and he is whispering to himself. I cannot understand what he is saying, of course. Is it a prayer? Has this native seen the light and found his way to God as his life slips away from him? It is not for me to question the most glorious actions of our Lord. Soon, the mutterings stop and the warrior's breath, rapid and shallow, begins to recede. An enormous amount of dark red blood continues to spill out of the gaping wound in his neck, running down his shoulder and into the designs that have been painted onto his chest.

I am still holding my dagger, stained with the warrior's blood, tightly in my right hand. It is as if I am somehow preparing for this doomed savage to miraculously rise up against me once more. Mercifully, after another moment or two, the warrior goes entirely still. His skin has been grotesquely marked with a mixture of fresh blood, brown dirt, and the crisp greenish-brown leaves of the forest floor. It is best for me to make my way back toward my men now, to reunite with my own Essex warriors. As I make my move, more quickly than I would anticipate given my weariness, I feel a strange energy surging inside of me. Something seems to be propelling me onward. It is as if I am walking upon the air.

Might I encounter more enemies on my journey to my men? Could I withstand another attack if it were to occur? I have no answers to the questions that flash before me. Instead, I shake them away and think back to the beginning of this conflict, to a time when I thought I would be bathed with glory for all I would accomplish in the name of the Lord. I do not regret the killing I have done on behalf of our merciful God and civilized man. I am simply doing my duty for Him and His Kingdom, as any honorable person would do.

Yet, I know now there is no glory in these accomplishments. There is no golden light shining down in my honor for what I have achieved. There has rarely been a moment in human history when the path of the righteous has been so clearly blazed against evil. As children of God, we know what we must do to make this land safe for Him in the name of progress. Those who were placed here before us are barring the journey forward that God intends for us. They are a test of our fortitude and endurance. This is our City on the Hill, and those who impede our advancement must be banished from our promised land, regardless of the cost.

There are some who support mercy toward the natives and claim to do so in God's name. Yet any mercy given to savages will only be repaid with blood and terror. I have seen it with my own eyes. They are the children of the devil and do not deserve our grace. I am not in search of honor here. I have shed blood. I have killed for the benefit of us all and for the hope that it will provide us with generations of prosperity to come. Such strength does not come naturally to us all, but those who have such gifts must fight in the name of those who cannot. It is the only way forward.

CHAPTER 9

Direct my footsteps according to your word; let no sin rule over me.

—Psalm 119:133

"Please, Ann, say something to me...."

My wife is sitting in her chair by the hearth as she stares vacantly into the flames. She is entirely still and does not even seem to blink her eyes. Unfortunately, such a condition is not new for her, but it seems to happen more often now than it once did.

"Say something to me, my dear. Please." I say this to her in a quiet voice as I sit beside her, hoping my tender cadence might jar her awake, that I might wrest her from her stupor. Despite my efforts, she offers no response.

"Please, come back to me, Ann," I continue, pleading in the same tone. "I need you, my dear."

I no longer hesitate to express my strongest feelings to Ann when she is in such a condition. It is not clear if she can understand me, or even if she can hear what I am telling her.

"I am begging you, Ann. It is Thomas. Please give me a sign, anything at all. Let me know that I have not lost you, my dearest."

Her silence endures despite my pleas. She is impervious to my commands, so I take a different tactic. "Do you remember our early days, Ann? When we lived by the Ipswich River after we had just been married?"

Engaging her memory can often bring her back to me more easily. At least it has done so before.

"Do you remember how the sunshine filtered so beautifully through the orange and red foliage on those crisp autumn mornings? Do you remember how we would wrap ourselves tightly in our quilt and marvel at the beauty God had laid before us?"

I am smiling now as I recall this fond memory. I am smiling without even realizing it. We hadn't a care in the world then. Everything had been set out before us to conquer.

"I think about those days often, Ann. I think about the songs that the meadowlarks sang to us. They were so delicate and melodic, my dear. It was as if they were singing their songs only to us. They seemed to have been sent from the heavens for our enjoyment. I marvel, still today, at such beauty in the world, Ann."

I press on amid my wife's continued silence. "How we loved those mornings together. It was just the two of us then. We had so much to live for, so much life ahead of us."

Ann continues to sit motionless before the fire, but I persevere in my attempt at reviving her.

"We were so young, our whole lives before us. It is a remarkable gift to have one's life ahead of them."

I pause for a moment, lost in my own thoughts and listening to the sounds of the crackling fire in the hearth.

"Please show me something, Ann," I say in my softest and gentlest voice. "Show me anything that will let me know you remember those days too, my dear, that you haven't forgotten what they meant to us."

Ann sits unblinking and vacant next to me.

"We would talk into the night then, spinning our dreams. You were so strong. I marveled at your strength and your purpose. I was transfixed by you, my dear."

Upon finishing my thought, I notice the slightest movement in Ann's face, first in her eyes and then, seconds later, her lips begin to quiver slightly.

"Are you trying to speak, my dear? Please, Ann, take your time. I am here, I am by your side, ready to hear what you have to say to me."

And then I can hear it. It is the faintest of songs, barely audible to my ears. It is the song that my wife used to sing to me often in her unusually high and delicate voice. She is singing it for me now.

> "... he in the folds of tender grass, doth cause me down to lie: To waters calm me gently leads restore my soul doth he: He doth in paths of righteousness for his name's sake lead me ..."

"Yes, Ann. It is the psalm you have always sung! You still remember it! Oh, how you sang it for me so beautifully, my dear. I will never forget how fortunate I was to have you sing this song to me. Keep singing, my dear. Keep singing your beautiful song in your sweetest voice! I cannot express how happy I am to hear it from you!"

The yellow bird is strikingly beautiful, despite her nefarious origins. Her feathers are as bright as the sun, so bright that my eyes hurt when I look upon her. She appeared on my windowsill this morning and has made her way through my open window and upon my bed, perching next to me where I lay.

"Do not deny what you know to be true, Anna."

I cannot tell if the yellow bird is speaking directly to me, or if I am simply aware of her words within my consciousness.

Whatever the case, I am certain that this bird is conveying a message to me, and I am listening.

"You deserve the pain you feel, Anna," she says. "You have not followed the path that has been set forth for you and so you must suffer."

I offer no response to the yellow bird's musings. Instead, I remain still and quiet upon my bed. After a moment or two of silence, the yellow bird suddenly begins to viciously peck at the tender skin between my fingers. Each harsh strike of her beak seems to be precisely calibrated to cause me the greatest amount of pain—pecking and pecking and pecking in a manner that is unbearable to me. Yet I can do nothing to protect myself or stop her. My body is entirely locked into place, and it seems the bird cannot be chased away.

"I am nourished by so many of them, Anna," the yellow bird tells me, as her feathers reflect the brightness of the morning sun painfully into my eyes. "There are hundreds here, but I know you are aware of that already. They have made their home here over many years, Anna. Soon, they will be entirely in control."

Suddenly, the yellow bird stops pecking at me, but my pain lingers on. We sit in silence. Soon, I began to take comfort in her presence. I begin to appreciate the yellow bird's power and how she wields it.

At the first sound of my door opening, the yellow bird quickly flies through my open window and into the tree in our yard. Father has come to check on me. I am grateful for his attentiveness and for the comfort he provides me now.

"You must eat, Anna," he says to me in a surprisingly sweet and soothing voice. "I have brought you some bread and some tea. Please have it now, my dear. It will help you regain your strength."

I am surprised by my father's caring actions. I want to be worthy of his concern and affection. I want to remain strong and shake off these troubles for his sake, if not my own.

"Thank you, Father," I manage in response to his kindness. I concentrate hard to ensure that the words come out of my mouth clear enough for him to hear and understand.

Sometimes my father sits with me at night when my state is often at its worst. He protects me from the darkness. He speaks to me tenderly in his reassuring voice. Sometimes he even strokes my hair, his fingers making their way carefully through my locks. His efforts give me hope, and I do my best to show him my gratitude.

"Do not speak, Anna," he always says to me when he sees me struggling to voice my appreciation to him. "Rest yourself, my dear. Rest is what you need the most now."

I do not tell Father everything, even in my moments of clarity, when it is easier for me to communicate with him. My experiences are far too terrible to burden others with—even *my own father. I want him to believe I am getting better. I want him to know that his tenderness is having its intended effect upon me. I want him to continue to care for me as he has been doing. He must not give up on me.*

CHAPTER 10

Slaves, be obedient to your human masters with fear and trembling, in sincerity of heart, as to Christ.
—Ephesians 6:5-8

John Indian is not supposed to be drinking spirits while he is tending to his duties at the ordinary. Yet we all know he does it with regularity, stealing quick sips of whiskey or rum when he thinks nobody is looking. I do not mind his drinking as much as some do. The spirits make John a more interesting conversationalist, loosening his lips in a way that would not be possible otherwise. In any case, none of us is willing to give away John's secret to old Nathaniel Ingersoll, regardless of what we think about his actions.

During our regular discussions at the tavern, which happen every few weeks or so, John and I address all manner of topics that, in truth, are mostly of little importance. We speak of our personal rivalries or of poetry or of how we should tend to our crops. Each of us seems intent on testing the other on his range of subjects. It is mostly all in good fun, but this evening's discussion is more serious. John is taking it upon himself—entirely unprovoked—to regale me with his own reading of our relationship with the native communities surrounding us. Given that John himself is an Indian, it is a subject we generally avoid discussing.

"The native will not yield to being a slave to the white man any longer, Thomas. It is not like it was before, during your grandfather's days."

I am allowing John to speak his mind without interruption. With his words flowing freely, I am better able to understand his reasoning, and more prepared for rebutting his argument. It is strange to me that a native who has spent his entire life toiling for the white man would make the case that the native does not wish to be in service to the white man. His reasoning has intrigued me, and I want to hear more about what John has to say on the matter.

"They decided during the great war of 1675 that they would fight at all costs," John says, the volume of his voice having increased as the evening has progressed, apparently in concert with the amount of spirits he has consumed. "They were not going to allow themselves to be taken as slaves like their fathers did before them."

"You mean to say that in spite of the clear advantages we had in weaponry, in strategy, in intelligence, and in tactics during the war, the natives chose not to yield to us because they feared enslavement?" I want to be certain I am hearing John's reasoning correctly.

"Yes. Fighting to their deaths was a better fate for them," John says with a grin of satisfaction upon his lips. "They vowed they would never give in again as their forefathers had."

Forcing captive heathen enemies into servitude is a longstanding tradition of honorable warfare, and not just for our own people. The natives themselves have been doing it since long before the white man ever stepped foot upon these shores. Yet John's obvious passion on this subject impresses me. He is emphatic about the matter, more emphatic than I have ever seen him while speaking about anything before.

"They vowed not to be sent far away from all that they knew," he says. "They were not going to be ripped from their homes and brought to Europe or the Caribbean or some other foreign land in chains. They would rather perish from an honorable death than suffer that ignoble fate."

During the war, Captain Lathrop told us that the native cannot help himself. He fights to the death like any rabid animal does, unable to control his emotions when they have been piqued. That is why the natives fight to the death—not because of a fear of benevolent servitude at the hands of civilized men. Yet I have tired of his argument and do not press John further, except to ask about his so-called wife.

"Has Tituba not thrived in our lands, John?" I ask. "Has her fate as a servant under the guidance of Reverend Parris not markedly improved her lot in life? And what of your own experience?" My anger builds as I ask my questions. I am surprised at how perturbed I have become at John's seeming disregard of facts he should well know.

"It is not easy," John says after a moment of thought. "We are grateful for what the reverend has provided to us, but nothing is so simple."

As my temper cools, I choose not to push any further. John's impertinence is likely a result of his intoxication. I should not fault him for it, given that I have chosen to look the other way at his drinking.

I cannot deny the savagery of that war: What I saw with my own eyes and participated in with my own hands was seemingly not of this world. The waves of fierce Wampanoag warriors still come at me in my sleep now and again, and Captain Lathrop's lectures about the nature of the Indian have remained with me these past fifteen years.

"John, you seem to forget that I fought in that war. I saw for myself the natives who yielded to our overwhelming strength. They did not all fight us to the death. There were many who saw the value of befriending the white man instead of fighting against him."

"Yes," John concedes. "I will grant you that there were some who gave in. I cannot deny that. Yet those who chose to yield did not believe the white man was the devil. They trusted him. They thought they would be treated honorably, that they would be respected for making the choice of laying down their arms. They did not fear the whites. That was their miscalculation."

"In that war," I say, feeling my ire build once again, "every man feared every other man: white, native; it did not matter. Trust was impossible and morality was entirely absent. God appeared to have forsaken all of us."

My intense response seems to capture John's attention. He is listening intently to me now, seemingly eager to hear what else I had to offer on this subject.

"The war debased everything it touched," I continue. "It stripped away all that was decent from any of us, leaving only raw and vile passions. We were all victims of the war's horrors. Every one of us. It would be easier to make the case that each of us had become a savage because of the war."

"I am listening," John says to show his respect and indicate his desire to hear more.

"The once-sacred rules of honorable warfare compel civilized men to show mercy toward captives and direct them toward the light of God. We must provide those who yield the respect they deserve for laying down their arms. We are meant to bless them with the knowledge of a new way of living and provide them with an opportunity for salvation, if such a thing might be possible for them. Those who yield to us should be given grace and shown the bounty of what their faithful servitude can provide."

"You are correct, my friend, but that is not the way of things any longer," John insists, this time with slightly less passion than before. "They will not yield as they once did."

John casts his eyes downward after speaking, as if he is ashamed of his argument now. It is as if he is afraid, given what I have said about my own gruesome experiences, to tell me that my thinking is misguided.

"Perhaps there are some who still believe in such things, Thomas," he concedes before trailing off.

"I do not doubt that some native servants are being kept as trophies by vain and selfish men who want nothing more than to make a spectacle of themselves and illustrate their supposed manliness," I tell John, hoping to smooth over what feels like tension that has arisen as a result of our discussion. "These individuals claim to tame the savage and domesticate the beast, yet there is no redemption for the wretched captives in such a case. Broken and humiliated, they have nothing to show for their honorable surrender but the degradation and indignity of being wholly subservient to another man."

I have hit my stride now and continue to lecture John on the topic: "In any civilized society, there will always be those who stand outside of what is expected of them. Progress will happen in its own time, as it always does, but you cannot say that this is the way of our world now. It is not so simple."

I will concede that John's argument is not entirely without merit, although I will not tell him as much. There are more than a few of us now who display a callous disregard for honor. Are those who flout these longstanding traditions simply ignorant of what they do, or is there some reasoning behind their actions? Have they been driven to such proclivities by the harshness of this land on which we live? We view the native as the savage, but are we, too, destined to succumb to our own savagery here? These thoughts swim uneasily within my consciousness, but I do not express any of them to John.

In truth, I am quite fond of John. He is as much one of us as anyone could expect a native to be. He has embraced our ways with much vigor, and he deserves our praise for doing so. He and Tituba are not among the class of captured natives. Instead, they have accepted our ways freely, throwing off the savagery of their origins.

Yet many here will always remain skeptical of John and Tituba. Perhaps they have good reason to be. The reverend claims Tituba has taken to the Word as strongly as anyone he has ever known. Still, she spoke of the devil with a gleam in her eye before the magistrates not long ago. I do not like to doubt the wisdom of Reverend Parris, but he would be the first to admit he is not infallible. I am anxious to know what John thinks about our present predicament, so I eagerly shift the course of our discussion.

"Do you believe those who have been accused of witchcraft here are purposely evil, or do you think they are ignorant of what they have done?"

"It is not for me to say," John replies more quickly than I expected.

"Certainly, you must have an opinion on the matter," I press.

"My opinion is of no matter. The result is still the same, is it not? What we must do in response to these events will not change. Is that not true?"

As he speaks, I can see that John is carefully searching for his words. He seems to want to ensure he will say something of which I will approve. I cannot deny my appreciation for such efforts. His willingness to conform his thinking to mine offers me some comfort.

"It is true, John," I say to reassure him. "And what you have said reminds me of a story."

Of the many stories I have exchanged with John at Ingersoll's, this is one I have never shared before.

"Years ago, I heard about a papist washerwoman in Boston who took it upon herself to torment the children of a good and pious family with her dark magic. This washerwoman was a keen practitioner of the devil's work, and she proudly wielded it as her means for afflicting these poor children. I cannot remember why she did it—or even if she admitted any reason for doing it at all. She was a worshipper of idols who could not speak more than a word or two of our language. It was said that she could not even recite the Lord's Prayer."

John's wide and expressive eyes betray his enthusiasm for my tale. Perhaps it is the drink, but he seems to have a particular affinity for stories about magic—especially stories about the white man's magic.

"She was a talented artist of magic and little else," I continue. "And while she was on the gallows, about to pay the ultimate price for her unthinkable sins against these poor, innocent children, this wretched woman proudly admitted to all who were present that her death would not end the girls' sufferings."

I take the opportunity to draw John deeper into the story.

"Can you imagine such a thing, John?" I ask him. Though I am hoping for a response, alas, he shakes his head slowly from side to side without a word. "This old wretch explained to all who were assembled that the poor children's terrible ordeal would continue, unabated, even after her imminent demise and descent into hell."

John looks at me with great anticipation, as if silently pleading with me to explain exactly how this evil woman conducted such magic—how it was that she could torment these children even after her death. Of course, I cannot give him an answer, though I relish experiencing his hunger for more.

"Unfortunately, her words proved to be prescient," I say. "The children saw no relief from their afflictions after her sentence was carried out. I am told they are still suffering by this woman's evil hand to this very day."

"How?" John finally utters in disbelief, seemingly unable to say more than that single word.

"That is not for me to say."

John wears his disappointment clearly upon his face, shaking his head in wonderment that a washerwoman could be capable of conducting such magic even from beyond the grave. He appears crestfallen at my inability to explain such a thing.

"We might not like to be reminded of it," I continue, "but the underworld is animated with dynamic forces that cannot be easily explained. There are many accomplices among us who are willing to soil their hands to obtain its benefits. They are eager to harness the potency of these dark arts for their own gain. You are quite right that their motives are of little importance to us now. We know that it is our duty to terminate this evil, regardless of how or why it has shown its face to us."

After a brief pause in our conversation, I return to my line of questioning about Tituba, eager to hear how John will respond.

"How does your wife know about this magic, John? Does Tituba really understand how the devil works and what his intentions are?"

John immediately casts his eyes downward and begins to shift uncomfortably on his feet. Does he fear I might find whatever answer he provides unacceptable? I cannot deny that I am deriving a certain pleasure from his discomfort. I imagine the thoughts that must be racing through his mind in this moment, the thousands of calculations he must be trying to make before responding. I know he will be careful not to hesitate for too long.

"I do not know what she knows, Thomas. She and I are not the same. We have lived different lives. We are not as similar as you might think we are, my friend."

As his words trail off, John turns his head away from me. Is it shame or fear he is feeling now? I cannot say for certain.

"We have an obvious choice to make," I reply. "We can choose to ignore the darkness we can see so plainly before us, or we can harness the light of God to banish it forever."

I am surprised when John responds to my statement.

"Perhaps Satan himself has introduced this complacency that you speak about, Thomas. Perhaps it has been building for generations, brick by brick. Perhaps we are only now seeing what has always been right before our very own eyes."

I am standing in a thick fog on the bow of a ship as it violently rocks upon a choppy sea. There is no land in sight, only the churning of rough waters in the tempest all around me. It feels as if the ship will be torn apart by the violent waves crashing against it. I can see nothing at all except for the heaving waters and the darkness stretching for eternity like an endless midnight. My legs seem as if they are about to give out beneath me.

I am entirely alone, yet I am never alone. There is a constant murmur: a cacophony of strange voices; a discordant humming that never entirely diminishes. The Black Man is almost always here, too, moving with his strange motions. What I would not give to be left alone now. He taunts me in his devious and clever manner. He is like an unscrupulous conductor, orchestrating the specters, choreographing their actions before me. He does his work with great subtlety. Is he Charon, guiding the spirits across the River Styx? Do the specters require such guidance?

I am far too frightened to think of anything useful while they haunt me. They seem to know precisely what they must say or do to induce my fears. They prod me like a misbehaving horse. I endure it as best I can. My only solace is knowing that they will leave me soon because they rarely stay for long. It is as if their time on this earth is fleeting, and they must use every second of it to torment me. Still, I am grateful for whatever it is that compels them to leave. They laugh at me in the most cruel and unfeeling fashion. They are amused by my fear, and they stoke it like a flame. They tell me I have been bad and that the devil will see me in hell. They tell me my only salvation is to sign his book so that he will spare me. They say I must enter a contract with Satan to save me from the eternal damnation I will soon face. I try to remember what I have seen, who it is that comes to me, but I cannot remember it all. There are far too many of them to remember.

I have vowed not to speak to the specters who haunt me. I try to endure their musings stoically, in silence, until they go back to the underworld or to wherever their hiding places are. I try to ignore them, but it is not always possible. They are too cunning for such a simple tactic. Sometimes I feel pinpricks over my entire body, often at the worst moments, when I am busy with my chores or tending to the children. It is the feeling of a million tiny needles being carefully inserted into my skin over and over and over. I do not see the specters or hear their voices, but every inch of me is overcome with pain until the discomfort is unbearable. Then, as suddenly as it began, the pain disappears, and I forget what it feels like until it happens again.

There are moments when my sight goes entirely dark or my hearing is completely silenced, only to return moments later. I am sometimes driven to such fits of nervousness that I can do nothing more than curl myself into a ball and hold myself until the episode has subsided. And then there are my moments of clarity—periods of pure bliss in which I can remember a time when I did not have to endure such torments. In these moments, I pray that the clarity will remain with me forever. Yet it always slips away again, sooner than I hope. It is far too fleeting, like sand slipping through my fingers.

I must be paying a price for some indiscretion I have committed, something I have done that has made me deserve such horrible suffering in the eyes of the Lord. Perhaps I have let the devil into my life unwittingly. Maybe I have given the devil a haven. Perhaps I have not prayed hard enough or have not been sincere enough in my devotion to the Lord. I have always believed that I have placed God before all else, but what if I am wrong? Perhaps it is the devil who has allowed me to feel this false sense of security. Perhaps I have been tricked into believing I am pious when I am not. I have always believed that I have fully given myself to the Lord's mercy, but perhaps that was never the case. How can I be sure of anything now? What must real devotion feel like if it is not what I have felt?

There are those here who barely mask their contempt for God. They mercilessly mock the mechanics of our devotion to Him without a care in the world. Such behavior has always appalled me, but perhaps I am the one who has been misguided. Perhaps those for whom I have felt contempt *are the ones who have embraced God as they should. It is I who has let the devil into my heart, not they. Have I always been heading down this dark pathway? Has everything I have believed been untrue?*

CHAPTER 11

With upright heart he shepherded them and guided them with his skillful hand.
—**Psalm 78:72**

We have not always had sound spiritual guidance in Salem. There is a history here of ministers who have not managed their affairs well. Reverend Parris, though, is a different kind of man. He is not so easily manipulated by petty scheming or frightened by challenges. He is his own man—strong and certain. He bargained hard for his position here, and he seems intent on serving us for many years to come.

I have made a point of getting to know the reverend. He visits my home often to pray with me for the health of my wife and daughter. Our discussions after these prayer sessions frequently go well into the night. This evening, we're talking about Reverend Parris's life before his arrival in Salem, when he was as a planter in Barbados.

"It was an entirely different world," he tells me. "It was equal parts remarkable and corrupting at once."

"What do you mean? You cannot make such a statement without elucidating upon it."

"After my father died, I thought being a sugar planter would be my vocation for life. I felt relieved, even, that the matter had finally been settled. I left Harvard and came to Barbados with a restful mind, but when I arrived there, I saw that things were not so simple."

Reverend Parris has not told me much about his life in the Caribbean. I lean in toward him as he speaks, eager to hear more.

"There were many plantations by then, far more than there had been when my family arrived on the island years ago, when I was a boy. My father had told me about all the men who were racing to the Caribbean to seek their fortunes, but it was of no concern to me. I was at Harvard. I was going to be a minister. Yet, when I made the decision to carry on my father's legacy in Barbados after he passed away, those fortune-seekers suddenly became my world. And I could not catch up with them. It seems I had little chance of success against them."

"And what about the work of harvesting sugar? It is difficult, is it not?"

"Indeed. Quite difficult. But the greatest challenge seemed to be securing the proper mix of laborers: the indentured, the slaves, the skilled free laborers. In truth, I was not good at such calculations—certainly not as skilled as my father had been."

"God has blessed us each with our own talents, Samuel. The Almighty is far too wise to allow us to be successful at everything we take on."

"Quite right."

"I have always wondered," I say, "when was it that you acquired Tituba and John?"

"It was during that time. It must be close to twenty years ago now, shortly after I had come back to Barbados to run my father's plantation. The island was awash with slaves by then. I had not recognized the place when I arrived; it was so different from how it had been when I was a boy. The arrival of new planters meant the need for an influx of laborers, and many had been imported from Africa. I needed to acquire some additional labor of my own to help with my domestic duties. That is when I acquired Tituba. I came into John later, just before I left the island."

I nod without comment, and the reverend seems intrigued by my silence.

"What are you not telling me, Thomas?" he asks with a sly smile. "You seem to be up to something."

"Nothing at all," I say, returning his smile. "It is only that I am particularly intrigued by Tituba now, given our situation."

"She was a girl of nine or ten years old back then, the child of a laborer who was owned by an acquaintance of my father in Bridgetown. I learned of her when I made inquiries about my necessity for a housekeeper."

After a brief pause, he continues speaking: "She was different from the others. She is of South American extraction—a native, not an African. I cannot deny that I was drawn to such a difference, yet I cannot explain why, exactly, that is the case, even now."

Reverend Parris pauses for a moment, as if in thought, before he says, "But that . . . that, look that she wears . . ." He shakes his head slightly as he trails off without any further comment. I do not respond. After a few seconds of silence, he continues.

"I sold them all before I left Barbados, all except for her. I wanted her to come with me to Boston. If I could not succeed as a planter in the Caribbean, I was going to try my hand as a merchant in Boston—to make my own way, outside of my father's shadow."

"And John?" I ask. "He was with you by then?"

"I acquired him just before I left," the reverend responds. "I knew I would need a good man to assist me in my endeavors."

"Tell me, Samuel, did they come with you willingly?"

"They had no choice."

"Of course. But were they pleased to be leaving the island and to be accompanying you to this new land?"

"I cannot say for certain," he replies. "But Tituba ... she has always seemed eager for whatever is put before her."

"What do you mean?"

"I suppose she was intrigued about coming to Boston," he says. "She seemed to have no family on the island, and she had taken to her duties well enough."

"Why did you choose not to sell her before you left for Boston, as you did with the others?"

"I do not know." Again, Reverend Parris shakes his head slightly. "But I could not even entertain the notion of letting her go."

After a brief pause, the reverend continues: "She is a good person, despite these recent events. She has been in my household for nearly two decades. She has become indispensable to Mrs. Parris. She is God-fearing and willing to live as we do. I have known this about her from the moment I met her when she was a child in Bridgetown. I would not have brought her to Boston—or to Salem, for that matter—if I felt otherwise."

"I am not suggesting anything untoward," I say reassuringly in response to his clipped tone. "I am simply a curious man wishing to understand the adventurous life of my friend."

"I will not deny that she holds a certain sway, Thomas," he says, in a softer tone now. "For a woman of her station, she wields a peculiar strength over us."

I nod slightly at the reverend's words before he continues.

"But I believe that it is nothing more than the lure of exoticism. I have seen such lusty desires go unchecked often in the Caribbean, but we have God's guidance here to keep us on the proper path."

"As well as your own wisdom, my good reverend," I say.

It is overcast and cool today as I walk to the meetinghouse. I have been going there on my own when I am able to—even on days when there are no meetings—so that I may reflect and pray. I am not certain it can help me now, but it gives me some comfort to be there, nonetheless.

As I walk slowly along the Andover Road, with my head cast downward so that others might not recognize me, a woman seems to suddenly appear walking next to me, her face obscured by a large, wide-brimmed hat. I am struck by her closeness, discomfited by it, even. There are some here who are uneasy about my affliction and unafraid to tell me so. And there are others who pity me and are eager to offer their compassion. I cannot say which is worse, but I do my best to keep clear of everyone so that I might not provoke any feelings at all.

I continue walking toward the meetinghouse with the mysterious woman in lockstep close beside me. Anxious that she will confront me at any moment, I first try to speed up and then, when that is unsuccessful, I try to slow down. She remains in rhythm with my steps regardless of my pace.

It cannot have been more than a minute, but it feels as if this woman has been with me for days. I finally muster up my courage to glance over at her. All I can see below her large, wide brim is a wrinkled chin strewn with strands of wiry gray hair.

Perhaps she is only walking, I tell myself. Perhaps I have become concerned about nothing at all. Yet just as I am about to convince myself that the person beside me is nothing more than an old woman going about her business, I hear a slightly muffled, yet unmistakable voice: "I know what you did, Ann. We all know what you have done."

I pretend for a moment that I have heard nothing and continue my journey, picking up my pace.

"You and those girls were fortune-telling. The so-called reverend's daughter is your ringleader, is she not?"

I can hear the voice more clearly now, but I choose to pretend nothing is happening. I continue walking faster as I near the meetinghouse.

"You can go to pray, my dear, but you must know that God will not hear you. He will ignore your pleas for mercy as He always has, Ann. He has forsaken you."

"Who are you?" I finally say in an abrupt and harried tone, unable to ignore the voice any longer.

"I am Goodwife Nurse, Ann, and I am here to provide you with guidance."

I am surprised to hear a response to my question, but I continue to speak my mind.

"You cannot be Goody Nurse because Goody Nurse is in jail. She is so sick that she can barely walk. Why are you telling me these lies? Who are you?"

The figure, still walking in unison beside me, responds immediately, but does not answer my questions.

"He provides for me, Ann. He can make me strong or infirm—whatever it is that I require in that moment. Do not let my bodily weakness fool you. It is only a ruse that I use to fool the weak-minded in this village."

I say nothing in response. Yet the voice continues: "You and your family will not win. You cannot beat me when I have his power behind me as I do. You cannot win when all you have is your weak and foolish Reverend Parris."

"Let me be!" I mutter under my breath as I walk quickly up the steps of the meetinghouse.

"You have started this storm, Ann," the voice continues. "It was your bad behavior that released it. You cannot stop it now. You will never be able to put an end to his power."

CHAPTER 12

Beloved, do not believe every spirit, but test the spirits to see whether they are from God, for many false prophets have gone out into the world.

—1 John 4:1

"Father, I have news."

Anna has taken to using this phrase when she has something to share with me. She tells me she has "news" as if she is trying to protect me from its unseemliness. Such an amiable and harmless word, her euphemism.

She is wearing a pensive look. Or is it a look of weariness? Perhaps it is both. Despite her sufferings, Anna has perseverance. She is more capable than even I have given her credit for.

"It was Goodman Corey."

It is no longer necessary for her to provide a more detailed preamble. My daughter needn't do anything more than relay the name to me in order for her to know that I will fully understanding the matter.

Giles Corey is a man of some means who carries with him an ungodly and obscene level of self-importance. Anna's revelation that he is committed to the underworld is hardly a surprise to me. Yet he has been as swept up in this fury as any of the rest of us have been. He even helped bring his own wife before the magistrates not long ago. Like any scoundrel, once he found himself faced with his own accusations, he did what he had to in order to save himself.

"He had a strange and unusual vibrancy about him, Father." As she speaks, Anna's mouth turns downward, as if this revelation has somehow caused her grave disgust or discomfort. "I have never seen him so full of life," she continues. "It was a vile thing to behold, Father. And the look upon his face ..." Anna trails off without further comment.

"What else did you see, my daughter?" I question Anna gingerly, hoping to gain a clearer understanding of Corey's behavior, but not wishing to push her too hard in the process.

"He seemed so light, Father," Anna says flatly as she stares into the distance. "It was as if he were decades younger."

I can hardly imagine the old coot frolicking about before Anna, delighting in his renewed spirit gained through his devilish dealings. I nod and encourage Anna to tell me more.

"It was his servant," she says.

I respond with an inquisitive look.

"Goodman Corey told me that he killed him," Anna explains. "He claimed that his servant was a thief and that he killed him for stealing."

"That is not news. I am aware of Corey's transgressions. Most of us are aware of them."

"There is more," she says with some hesitation in her voice. "The servant was ... he was *with* Goodman Corey."

"What do you mean?"

"The servant was wrapped in a quilt upon my bed. He was there with the specter of Goodman Corey. The servant was ... was ... pursuing me."

"Pursuing you? How was he pursuing you?"

"I am not sure, but Goodman Corey seemed to be preventing him from harming me in some way. Goodman Corey's specter commanded me to write my name in the devil's book using my own blood or else he would be powerless to stop his servant's pursuit of me."

Anna's words spill out of her with great speed. It is as if she is trying to rid herself of the distress that they are causing her. Her growing anguish is more evident with every syllable.

"He produced a large volume, and he assured me that it was the devil's book. I could see from the strange writing on its cover that—"

Anna stops speaking and takes a deep breath. She seems to be incapable of saying more, evidently taxed by these revelations. In a moment, after closing her eyes and taking several deep breaths, she slowly begins again with a renewed determination.

"He begged me, Father," she says with a tremble in her voice. "Goodman Corey was pleading with me to sign that contract with the devil. He was sobbing before me, wailing horribly, with tears streaming down his cheeks."

I do not respond to Anna's revelation, but my eyes plead for her to tell me more.

"The servant was moving toward me from underneath the quilt on my bed. He was inching closer to me, as Goodman Corey begging me to sign the devil's book or else the man would have his way with me. He was crying, Father, and through his tears, Goodman Corey told me that he could no longer hold his criminal servant at bay. He said the man was sure to attack me in the most unholy manner and that my inaction would enable him to do so. Goodman Corey said I had emboldened this man with my wretched behavior."

I stare at Anna, entirely transfixed, but unable to speak.

"All I could think of doing, Father, was close my eyes. So, I closed my eyes as tightly as I could, and I waited for the servant."

I swallow hard as sadness overcomes me.

"I did not sign the book, Father. I am sure that I did not do it!"

"I believe you, Anna," I respond with much sympathy. "I believe you."

It is all that I can muster under these circumstances. Lord, give me the strength to do what I must do.

"She is in the devil's thrall, Anna."

Mercy is particularly animated as she speaks about Mary Warren. They are of similar age and vocation—both about eighteen and maidservants—and Mercy counts Mary among her friends. That seems to be why Mercy is particularly shaken by this news.

"She came to me soon after she saw the vision of Goodman Corey," Mercy tells me in an excited tone. "She was so frightened by it and did not know what to do. I told her she must speak to her master or mistress. They would know what to do and how to make a complaint against Corey to the magistrates."

Mary works in the home of John and Elizabeth Proctor, who are among the wealthiest families in all of Salem. Yet Goodman Proctor seems not to have taken well to Mary's news.

"She told me that Proctor did not believe her," Mercy says, speaking at a very harried pace, "and that he forced her to work at her wheel. He told her that if he witnessed one of her

fits, he would not help her, that he would beat her. He said she might burn in a fire or drown in a well for all he cared."

"How awful," I say, before expressing my own gratitude about my father's concern for my condition. "I am thankful that he believes me and wishes to see me get well," I tell Mercy.

"You are fortunate, Anna," she says. "God bless your father. I am grateful to him as well."

"What can we do for poor Mary?" I ask Mercy.

"She will not speak to me now," Mercy says. "But I have heard some disturbing news from Goodwife Sibley. I am not certain if it is true or not."

"Goodwife Sibley always places herself at the center of everything," I say.

Mercy nods in agreement before continuing. "She says Mary has left a note on the meetinghouse door for Reverend Parris. And that he took the note and then questioned Mary."

"What did the note say?" I ask.

"I am not aware of its entire contents, only what Goody Sibley has told me about the letter."

"What did she tell you?"

"Only that the note contained a message about the afflicted persons being untruthful," Mercy says.

"Untruthful?" I respond. "Is Mary not afflicted herself?"

"That is why I have said that she is in the devil's thrall, Anna," Mercy says, her voice enthusiastic. "It makes no sense *that she would say such a thing about those who have been afflicted, given her own condition. I have seen the devil's deviousness. He is always hard at work to win us over in all manner of ways. I fear that poor Mary is in his grip now."*

CHAPTER 13

Be sober, be vigilant; because your adversary the devil, as a roaring lion, walketh about, seeking whom he may devour.

—**1 Peter 5:8**

"I have been very wicked. I hope that I shall be better."

It appears that Abigail Hobbs does not see fit to lie to Judge Hathorne as many of the others have. She is but fifteen years old, perhaps not yet skilled enough in the art of deception, like so many of her kindred are.

"He said he would give me fine things if I did what he would have me do," Hobbs explains.

She is speaking of her time on the eastern frontier. It is an unruly and godless place. Perhaps it has been forsaken entirely by the Almighty. It seems that the devil has found fertile ground in the wilds of Maine.

"And what would he have you do?" Judge Hathorne asks Hobbs in a steady voice.

"Why, he would have me be a witch."

"And did you sign the devil's book?"

"Yes, I did. But I hope God will forgive me."

The judge's faithful assistant Jonathan Corwin is furiously scribbling notes at Hobbs's revelations. She is the devil's helper for certain—she is admitting as much before us all now. Yet her candor will only bolster our cause. She does not have the cunning of Rebecca Nurse or Sarah Osborne or the others who so readily deny what we all know to be true. Like Tituba before her, Hobbs's simplemindedness is yielding the perfect truth. As Hathorne continues his examination of her, the meetinghouse is as silent as the grave.

"Who do you hurt?" he asks her.

"Mercy Lewis and Ann Putnam."

"What did you do to them when you hurt them?"

"I pinched them."

"How did you pinch them? Do you go in your own person to them?"

"No."

"Does the devil go for you?"

"Yes."

I have heard Anna's cries of pain and calls for mercy. Were these the result of Hobbs's handiwork? Who else goes about in this way to trouble her?

"Did you know Sarah Good was a witch when you saw her?" Hathorne is probing more deeply now.

"Yes," Hobbs replies.
"How did you know it?"
"The devil told me."

I am tending to the chickens when I see him walking down the path toward the farm. John Willard has an unusually long gait and holds himself in such an erect and sturdy manner as he walks that he is easy to notice from a great distance. I think for a moment about going inside so that I might avoid any confrontation with him, but I choose to remain busy with my chores instead. I will face whatever is to come.

"Good morrow, Anna," he says as he approaches me. His voice is unexpectedly kind. I return his greeting as unaffectedly as I can muster, yet I am anxious by his presence before me.

"I have come to see you again. I hope you are feeling better." John says this with genuine concern, in a voice that makes him seem more tender than his large physique would suggest.

"I am managing, thank you, constable."

John Willard had visited in the weeks after my affliction. He had been eager to know about my condition.

"I am glad to hear this," he says. "I have been praying for your return to health, and for the others' health as well."

"I am grateful for your prayers."

It was some two years ago when John Willard came to our door and offered his services to our family. He was new to Salem, and Father eagerly accepted his offer, given our great need for help at the time. Baby Sarah had just been born and she was quite a sickly child. Mother needed all the assistance she could get, and John Willard seemed to be sent to us from the heavens.

"Anna, I am wondering if I might have a word with you. I do not wish to be cross with you. I have always been so fond of you, but . . ." He trails off and pauses for a moment before proceeding again. He seems to be thinking about what to say. "I'm afraid that I have heard rumors, Anna, from Goodman Knight and others. They tell me you are saying that I have tormented you, that I have come to you like a witch and done harm to you."

I am surprised at how direct he is and unsure how to respond to his accusations. I like John Willard. I have liked him from the first moment I saw him at our door some two years ago. He was always so careful and nurturing with Sarah, and he never once treated me with anything but kindness. Yet I cannot deny what I have seen these past few days, the way in which his specter has haunted me so.

"I wish I could say it was not true, John. But I am obliged to report what I have witnessed." I am barely able to keep my voice from cracking as I speak.

"But, Anna," he says with a sudden urgency, "I would never hurt you—you know that. I would never do anything to torment you in any way. We have always gotten along so well. When I was here with you and your family, we . . ." John stops speaking, seemingly incapable of continuing his thought any further.

"I am very sorry, but I must report what I know to be true. It is my duty to do so." I say this in as gentle of a voice as I can muster under the circumstances. I do not wish to be anything but kind to this man, even if I am aware of his true nature.

"How can you believe in your heart that I would harm you?" he asks. "I ask you now, as God is my witness, how can you believe that I am capable of doing such a thing to you?"

My only response is to cast my eyes downward and shift nervously upon my feet. After a few moments of silence, John speaks again, his soft voice returning. "I am so sorry for the loss of baby Sarah. I tried everything I could do to keep her vibrant and to save her. I grew to love that child. God rest her soul."

I remain silent and continue to keep my eyes cast toward the ground as emotion wells up inside of me. My eyes begin to fill with tears.

"I am sorry you feel that you must make these accusations against me," he says. "I hope God sees to it to improve your condition. Regardless of what you think of me, I wish only for you to be well again."

"Fare thee well, constable," I say, though I can hardly manage to utter these few words before quickly turning toward the house and bursting into tears.

CHAPTER 14

JUNE 1667

THE PUTNAM FARM NEAR THE IPSWICH RIVER

Twenty-five years earlier

That with their miseries they opened a way to these new lands; and after these hardships, with what ease other men came to inhabit them.

—**William Bradford,**
Of Plymouth Plantation

"Be sure that your pack is fully stocked, Thomas. You can expect to be gone the entire day, perhaps longer."

"Yes, Father," I reply. I can hear the excitement in my own voice. I had expected him to ask me one day, but I was not prepared for it to happen now. When I heard his words this morning, I nearly jumped out of my skin. I am sure Father must have noticed my exuberance, but I was grateful he did not scold me for it. I cannot help but be proud he has seen fit to enlist me for such an important duty. It is real work for a real man. We are to open our land for crops. It is a complex and challenging undertaking, and Father needs all the assistance he can get. I am glad to be of service to him, to earn my keep as a Putnam.

A pulse of excitement surges through my body as we set off on the journey just before dawn breaks, loaded down with our tools and equipment, and ready for a long day of hard work together, just the two of us. I have never felt more important in my life. My father has often told me that we carry a substantial responsibility. As founders of this land, we bear a great burden, he says. I can feel that responsibility now, in this moment. Perhaps I am feeling it for the very first time.

It is not long before I recognize, however, that Father's true purpose for this adventure goes far beyond the job of clearing our land for crops. It seems that Father's primary goal is something else entirely—something more specifically focused on me.

"The Indian is not a savage," my father says to me, as if pulling the phrase out of the air as we are walking.

"I see," is all I can muster in return, barely able to disguise my confusion at his strange utterance.

Father excels at many things, but conversation is not one of them. Perhaps he is not comfortable introducing the real purpose of our journey, or perhaps his opaque messaging is part of what he has had in mind all along. His stoic manner and hearty disdain for the trivial musings that accompany most discussions often hinder my father's ability to communicate. It occurs to me that he might even have made the deliberate choice of surprising me with his declaration about the natives. Perhaps it is an ambush of sorts.

"You must understand, son, that such simple thinking risks everything we have gained here," he continues.

"I am listening," I offer to encourage him. "Tell me more."

Father retains a solemn manner as he speaks. His musings are so grave and serious that it feels almost as if he is in mourning as he speaks. Today, his usual austerity has been replaced by something even heavier and more brooding. There is a substantial weight to his words and a depth of emotion I have not witnessed from him before.

"The natives have been placed on our land by God to test our courage and our commitment to Him and the path He has set before us," my father tells me.

"But how are we being tested?" I eagerly respond.

"We are not meant to ask such questions, Thomas," he tells me. "Our ability to shine light on God's glory was never meant to be an easy task. If it were, then our righteous cause would not be as worthy as it is."

My father continues making a variety of revelations about the natives during our walk to the site that we are meant to clear. Even after we reach our destination and begin our strenuous work in the thick heat of the forest, my father reveals much more than I thought he, or anyone else, knew about the native people who are spread out across our lands. He is more verbose than I have ever known him to be before, providing intricate details and musings about seemingly insignificant and trivial matters related to the native peoples. Characteristics that are so often dismissed or ignored, he carefully explains in vivid detail.

"A keen knowledge of the inner workings of their hearts and minds is what holds the key to our survival," he tells me. "God has intended for us to know these details in order for us to thrive here. It is our sacred duty to solve the enigma that the natives represent rather than to turn dismissively away from it."

"How can we achieve this?" I ask. "How can we know such details?"

"The Almighty, in His infinite mercy, has bestowed enormous intelligence upon us, son," he tells me. "It is our duty to use what He has blessed us with to our own advantage."

I do my best to mimic Father's dignified manner and listen closely to his words, responding only when I have a genuine query.

"You are a future leader in our community," he tells me with a hint of pride in his voice, "and thus I am obliged to equip you with deep knowledge and cultivate within you a strong willingness to understand."

I swell with pride at my father's words, but strive to remain austere, knowing he would frown upon a haughty display.

"This knowledge will bring you power, son," he explains. "You must understand the ways of the Indian so that you might gain an advantage over him and ensure the survival of our God-fearing race."

I can manage little more than a grim nod at such solemn and important words.

"Too many of us are content with seeing the Indian as nothing more than the counterpoint in a duality of good versus evil," my father says. "But men like us must have our wits about us, so that we may exploit their weaknesses more fully."

"I will do as you say, Father," I tell him with sincerity. "I wish to learn as much as I can."

I have studied my father for all fifteen years of my life, yet I have found it difficult to fully understand him. He is a stern and serious man. I do not believe I have ever seen him smile or laugh, not even one time. He carries much too heavy of a burden for such frivolity. His responsibilities as a pillar of this growing community overpower any opportunity for levity. His father before him came to this region and established himself among its most important families. Father has taken the responsibility bequeathed to him by his own father quite seriously. Yet I believe that he relishes living such a life. I can see it reflected upon his face and in the way he conducts his business. It shows itself in his deliberate actions. It is as if he is playing a part in some great performance where his character must remain solemn and sturdy throughout, come what may.

 I cannot deny that I am in awe of my father. In fact, I fear him, often. He does not treat me poorly. That is not why this fear lives within me. But like any son, I do not wish to disappoint him. I admire how his resolve and determination provide him with sustenance. I appreciate how his sense of purpose and responsibility propel him forward. Yet I remain skeptical that I will be as driven and purposeful as he is.

 In truth, I fear what my father's stern demeanor portends for my own adulthood. Must I, too, carry the weight of the world upon my shoulders? Is that to be my own lot in life? Will the concerns that I carry with me obscure any possibility for lightness in my existence? The heft of his words is substantial, but I suppose this is what being a man is meant to be. One has no choice but to pass along wisdom. As his eldest son, it is my duty to carry the burden of this knowledge and continue its journey through the generations, whether I wish to or not.

"We do not take the threat of the natives as seriously as we should, Thomas," Father continues. "Do not make the same mistake others have made. We cannot afford to be complacent about such matters."

"I understand," I say to reassure him that I am listening closely before asking how such knowledge will provide us with an advantage.

His answer is not so simple.

Father's beliefs about the natives are more complex than most. I have been aware of this fact for as long as I can remember. He has worked hard to ensure, from our youngest age, that his children recognize his way of thinking. My father is not given to simple dogma as many others are. Still, my query is sincere. How can such knowledge provide us with an advantage over the Indian? If I am being honest, the natives stir an uneasiness within me. I am not fearful about our ability to ultimately prevail over them, if that is what God asks us to do. Instead, my concern, such as it is, relates to how the native carries himself in the world. He is nothing like we are, and I fear that all of the knowledge in the world will not fully illuminate his darkness.

A few months ago, while hunting for rabbits near our farm, I came across a young native woman gathering firewood. She wore only a loose deerskin covering that exposed much of her upper body, including her breasts. She appeared to be sixteen or seventeen years old and possessed long, lean muscles in her arms and legs that enabled her to easily carry several substantial logs without much difficulty at all.

Upon seeing this girl, I swiftly hid behind a bush and readied my musket. Though I was not expecting the need for an attack, I wished to prepare myself in case there were others about who wished to do me harm. The girl continued with her work, adeptly scanning the forest around her with her keen vision. Then, after she seemed to have gathered all the firewood she needed, the girl turned back in the opposite direction and began walking away from where I was hiding.

After taking a step or two away from me, while I remained well-concealed within my hiding place, the girl suddenly stopped dead in her tracks and turned her head back in my direction. After a second or two of silence, she whistled loudly in a clear and sharp tone. Startled, I immediately broke into a run in the opposite direction of her, as fast as I was able to go. Only a few steps ahead, my foot got caught in some brush and I stumbled unheroically to the forest floor. When I looked up again, the native girl was suddenly standing but a few steps away from me. She let out a hearty and scornful laugh. Her chortle could be heard echoing loudly against the trees around us. It seems the native girl had been aware of my presence the entire time.

Despite my being hidden, armed, and ready to strike at a moment's notice, she hadn't felt the slightest bit of concern.

It is impossible to see how we will not one day clash with our strange Indian neighbors in some great battle for our New Jerusalem. Ministers preach endlessly about such conflict from the pulpit—a fight between good and evil, they tell us. Such simple thinking makes it easier for us to dismiss the natives as unknowable and unworthy of our vigor, my father would say.

"Might such knowledge about the native encourage us to debase ourselves as they have done, Father?" I am willing to ask more questions now, emboldened by his growing faith in me.

"Such thinking is what they desire from us," he tells me. "When we hold such beliefs, we are playing the devil's game."

Father has worked tirelessly to imbue others with his unique thinking about the natives. He is clever about this business, though, careful to do it with subtlety and finesse so as not to be seen as fanatical. Yet it seems that his crusade has fallen mostly upon deaf ears. Even those who respect my father often ignore his pleas to understand the native people more completely. Now, it seems, Father is entrusting me to keep this flame burning as part of my own legacy.

As we toil away in the forest, clearing the bush bit by bit, Father speaks to me in such an open manner that I am beginning to view him differently now. I suspect he might be measuring my responses, perhaps so that he might punish me later for not acting as I should. As the day progresses, though, I become more certain of his sincerity. I am moved by his unique passion and his desire to instill it within me.

"The native is an intricate being, Thomas," my father tells me. "Much more complex in nature than we often give him credit for."

Father goes on to explain details about the ways of the natives—how and to whom they worship, how they treat one another, what pushes them to war and brings them back to peace. He speaks about their relationships—between their leaders and their common people, between husbands and wives, between fathers and sons. He tells me about their notions of property, what foods they consume, how they cultivate their crops, and who they honor and despise. No topic is ignored; no subject is forbidden.

Later in the day, I feel myself opening up to this new way of interacting with my father, and I become bolder and more inquisitive.

"I have never believed in the idea of introducing the heathens to God," Father tells me. "It will only bring their inherent evil directly into the church and provide them with another means for infiltrating us." After a brief pause, my father continues. "Showing them the light of God and allowing them to carry on as if they are a civilized people is antithetical to everything that we hold dear, Thomas," he says. "Their unclean views cannot be so easily washed away."

Their only true path forward, Father tells me, is through submission and annihilation. "The natives must be destroyed," he says to me in a flat and unfeeling tone. "Their only hope for survival is as a neutered and defeated people, in complete subjugation to our own superiority."

"Eventually," Father explains, "they will be extinguished entirely from this land and lost to history, just as the Lord has intended them to be."

Once this occurs, my father assures me, we will have our City upon the Hill.

I listen to my father's dramatic words without comment. It is as if he is a player upon a stage offering his soliloquy to the gathered masses or a dynamic preacher singing the praises of the Almighty.

"I am as repulsed by the ways of the Indian as any among us are, Thomas," he suddenly says to me. Perhaps he is wishing to recalibrate his words so that I will not mistake his lusty zeal for admiration.

"My enlightenment on this matter was born out of a simple desire to bring the natives to heel," he says. "And to accomplish this victory, son, we must overcome our outward loathing of our enemy. Such feelings do not serve our purposes well."

"How did you come to this way of thinking, Father?" It is a question that has been on my lips since long before we headed into the forest this morning.

"My study began at a very young age," he explains. "I studied the native as some might study the Word, often doing so behind the back of my own father. He feared that I might become too comfortable with the ways of the native, too enamored by them as others have been guilty of doing in the past." Father assures me that I needn't harbor such a concern myself. "It is my sincerest wish that you gain the knowledge that you must know about the native, my son."

"And how were you able to become so knowledgeable about the Indian, Father?"

"While I was still a young man I came upon a native, nearly my own age, foraging for food alone in the forest one day. He was bare-chested in the late-springtime air and his dark hair was shorter than my own."

As Father shares his tale, I try to imagine his encounter with this strange native, but I find it impossible to conjure up the picture in my mind.

"He wore no markings on his delicate face or body. Had he been wearing the clothes of a civilized man, I might not have recognized him as a native at all."

"Did he see you?" I ask.

"I did not think so. At least not at first. But I felt compelled to monitor him for as long as I was able to. I wanted to observe him in his natural environment so that I might learn more about the ways of his people."

Eventually, my father explains, he met this native and learned that he was called Quinnapin. Father does not tell me how he met him, and I do not feel capable of asking him for such details, in spite of my newfound openness with him. Perhaps Quinnapin had caught sight of my father eyeing him and gave chase. Or perhaps my father had been the one who chased down Quinnapin, tackling him onto the forest floor. I do not know his reasoning for keeping this information to himself, but Father explains to me that he had observed Quinnapin for some time as the native closely examined the surrounding foliage with a careful eye, picking a variety of berries, flowers, and leaves. He tells me how the native would carefully inspect each one before placing it into a small basket that he carried nimbly upon his arm.

"It was clear that he had a keen knowledge of the land but not the instincts of a fighting man," Father says. "He was a thoughtful and contemplative man, not like the natives I had dreamed up within my consciousness."

I can hear the admiration in my father's voice as he recalls his memories of this native. I wonder if he is stifling his feelings for my sake or if he wishes for me to witness such emotion?

"We had some difficulties communicating, at first," my father explains. "But I was surprised at how quickly we were able to make ourselves understood to each other."

"What did you talk about?"

"Quinnapin spent a great deal of time eagerly answering my numerous queries," he explains. "He was quite careful and reflective in his responses to me, giving much focus and thought to them."

It seems that this native wished to be certain that my father understood him fully and that he was not taking some distorted meaning from their interactions.

As Father continues to tell me about Quinnapin, I notice a hesitation within him. He seems to be turning a thought over in his mind, perhaps wondering if he should reveal something to me. After a moment or two, he begins to speak again, clearly choosing his words carefully.

"I had wondered for a long time if a savage could be truly capable of real introspection," he says. "I began to wonder if I might have been party to some kind of performance from Quinnapin. Perhaps he was a player performing solely for my benefit. I wondered if I might have been a dupe in the middle of a ruse?" Father's face sours as he speaks these words, as if he is recalling some bitter and painful memory. "Such ignorance . . ." he mutters almost inaudibly.

My father does not reveal very much about what he and Quinnapin discussed during their time together. Perhaps he does not feel the need to discuss such specifics with me. Or perhaps, even after all these years, he still wishes to keep their intimacies to himself. Yet as he is speaking, my father seems to use every word to implore me to acknowledge that the native is a worthy and dangerous adversary who cannot be underestimated. There is an urgency to his message that is disquieting to me. His words seem to be some sort of calculated plea—every phrase an attempt to win me over to his side.

"We learned a lifetime of knowledge about each other," my father tells me in an almost wistful tone. "Quinnapin was an exceptionally keen observer of the land. He possessed many lifetimes worth of knowledge about the herbs, vegetables, and fruits growing in our region, some of which I had not even been aware of then."

Because he was not a warrior, my father tells me, Quinnapin knew very little about the Wampanoag ways of fighting.

"He seemed to have been shunned by the warriors," Father says, "perhaps cast out for some unseemly or cowardly behavior. But he was not like other natives, Thomas. Many are so quick to temper and ready for a fight, but Quinnapin did not seem to have such traits about him."

It seems that my father took full advantage of Quinnapin's unique knowledge and his eagerness to share it with others. "With each session together over many months," Father explains, "Quinnapin became increasingly animated. He seemed to recognize the rareness of opportunity he had to explain the intricacies of his people and their relationship to the land. He seemed to relish being my teacher and I was keen to take advantage of his pride. I did not wish for any ill feelings to disrupt the flow of information that Quinnapin was providing to me, so I would simply nod and ask questions to clarify his meaning. As soon as we had finished our meetings, I would scribble what I could remember into my notebooks."

It is difficult to imagine my father as a young man, nearly my age, feverishly scratching down his recollections from Quinnapin's musings. But I have learned much that I never knew about him today and I revel in this unexpected vision of him.

"It was Quinnapin's duty to locate sources of food and medicine for his people," my father explains to me. "I learned much by listening, son, and encouraging him to speak more."

As my father continues to regale me about the intricacies of the various foods and herbs, I cannot help but notice his own pride in action. Perhaps he is speaking to me now as Quinnapin had once spoken to him, carefully relaying every minute detail of knowledge.

After several months of visiting Quinnapin at regular intervals, my father says that he abruptly ended their meetings entirely. "We had never been seen together by anyone—native or white—and I wished to be assured that it would remain so," he explains. "I could not risk facing the prospect of more rumors about consorting with heathens. Too many of us are easily seduced by the natives, enchanted by them in ways that are unforgivable. I had no intention of being accused of such wretched behavior."

My father seems to shift his tone now as he begins to explain his final interactions with his native acquaintance, speaking more solemnly. "Each time that the two of us parted," he says, "I shared a handshake with Quinnapin."

It was apparently a custom of which the natives had no knowledge. Yet it seems that Quinnapin soon became eager to take part in this new ritual, anticipating the handshake as their sessions together were winding down. I cannot help but imagine the difficulty my father must have had in witnessing such a display, given his disdain for even the slightest show of emotion. But perhaps he was different then.

"At the conclusion of each handshake," my father says, "Quinnapin would break into a broad grin and say: Until next time, my friend."

I do not ask my father if he returned Quinnapin's sentiment. I can imagine the shame and disgust that Father must have felt at such a frivolous display of affection. I can envision him now breaking off the handshake abruptly and fleeing into the forest without a sound, hoping to outrun such an overwrought display of emotion.

Yet, as my father speaks to me about Quinnapin, his wistful look remains. Perhaps it is the memory of his youth. Or perhaps his emotion is derived from the promise that those days had given to him. It is clear that Quinnapin lingers with my father, still today.

"He was a good man," my father says after pausing for several minutes, seemingly spent now from his physical and verbal excretions.

The two of us remain silent during our long walk home.

CHAPTER 15

There is no peace for the wicked.
—Isaiah 48:22

Existing among those who wish us ill has always been fraught with struggle. Our ancestors were brave to come here, but we are braver still to thrive as we do among these people, to be an enemy to the savages yet forced to live by their side. Such circumstances must be our truest test from God.

There is always trouble with the natives, but we are safer now than we were during the war, some decade and a half ago. The raids came more regularly then—women and children were seized and forced to endure an unspeakable hell on Earth at the soiled hands of our enemies. Our strong hand after the war has lessened such atrocities, but we will likely never be immune from the cowardly attacks of those opportunists. We do not have the luxury of complacency. Yet our steadfast resolve will win the day; I am certain of it.

One cannot be so sanguine about the wilds of the eastern frontier. The Province of Maine is surely forsaken by the Almighty, if not by the fortune-seeking scoundrels who run there. For those who choose to live in such a place—prospecting for wealth and whatever opportunities they can get their hands on—fear and vigilance are constant companions. Raids and attacks are a regular occurrence there.

As an infant child, Mercy Lewis's family was viciously attacked on the frontier. It was an unprovoked and unmanly fight, typical of that place. Somehow, they managed to survive. The natives seem to relish taking advantage of their greater numbers in Maine, marauding as they see fit, setting upon those who are simply going about their business and living a God-fearing, hardworking existence. Those who settle on the frontier have come to accept this challenging life, I suppose. I have heard from those who have been to the frontier that the situation is improving; some say they will soon have it subdued entirely. I have no reason to believe such a thing.

Not long ago, when Mercy was only a year or two older than Anna is now, her community in Maine was attacked again by a group of plundering savages. Anyone with half a mind could have predicted there would be another attack. This time, however, her family was not spared. I had warned them of their vulnerabilities when they came to live in Salem after their first run-in with the natives, but they were determined to return to that place, claiming the rumors of imminent attack were unfounded. "We are gaining ground upon them," they wrote in their letters. "God is smiling upon us. We have them on the run." One must never forget that a wounded animal is always the most dangerous.

I shudder to think what my own destiny might have been had I not dissuaded my wife of her desire to run to the frontier. It was a crude and thoughtless notion, but in the early years of our marriage, when her troubles were just beginning, it had become her own, singular obsession. She wanted to run away from the confines of our village to remake her life—our life—in that wretched wilderness. She seemed to believe she could find refuge from her troubled mind there, to free herself from its burden, or at least shelter herself among the unknown.

"Think of it, Thomas," she told me then. "We can start fresh and build a new life together, a life that is all our own."

Despite her passion for the idea, I was unconvinced of its merits. Those who choose to run to the frontier are often the most artless and headstrong among us. They are too occupied by their own delusions—of success, of freedom, of wealth—to recognize how to make a decent life in the world. They are blinded by the luring shine of gold that dangerously blots out the realities of such a forsaken land. Thankfully, God rewards us for our knowledge. I am well aware of the truths that exist on the frontier. I could not, in possession of such knowledge, take my wife and raise my family in such a place, no matter how much Ann wished for me to disregard my own thoughtful reasoning and throw caution to the wind.

"If you do not take me, Thomas," she threatened, "I will go on my own. I will go without you, and you will never see me or hear from me again. You will be disgraced. You will be humiliated before all the people of this village. Do you want that? Is that your wish for your great legacy?"

Those were dark times for us; there is no denying it. Still, I held fast to my firm beliefs.

"You will not run, Ann," I argued. "You cannot do it and survive. You cannot make it there without me. You will be a crazed woman who has abandoned her family. Is that what you want? You will be the mad outcast who has fled to the edge of the kingdom all by herself. You will be ridiculed and despised. You will be shunned."

Even in those early days, I knew that her unsettled consciousness was pressing this matter upon her like a Moxon vise. Today, many years later, I am still not fully aware of Ann's true feelings on this matter. Back then, she was a frightened young woman trying to outrun her terrible troubles the only way she thought she could. Those days were not easy for us, but the days that came after them have proven harder still.

There have been many times since then when I have feared she has left, many times when I have been awoken with a start, pulled from my bed by a nightmare about some doomed and feeble attempt she has made to flee. For a moment, before I can see her beside me in our bed, I shudder at the thought of my helplessness, quiver at the notion that there is nothing I can do to save her, that it was too late for us, that even if she is found, she would be lost.

In my dream, some marshal would approach me with a solemn look upon his face.

"Sergeant Putnam," he would say, "we were surprised to come across Goodwife Putnam in the forest, quite far from the village. You can rest assured that she is safe, sir, but I am afraid I cannot say she is quite well...."

I am grateful that Ann has remained with me. Despite how her vexed consciousness has tormented and taunted her, she has not run away, at least not yet. The Almighty has kept her safe, and I pray that He continues to do so.

Yet I cannot help but wonder now if Ann was correct in her thinking back then. Perhaps I was too hasty in squashing that notion of hers. Might we have been able to outrun our troubles and make a life for ourselves among the savages? I cannot deny that I sometimes wonder what might have happened had we tried such an adventure.

Only God knows the answer now.

"It did not seem real, Anna."

Mercy appears before me, beautiful and bright as always, her voice as clear as a bell. Her face is as calm and gentle as ever, in spite of her harrowing story.

"It was as if it were happening within my own wild imagination—some inconceivable nightmare replaying within my consciousness. I had never expected it to happen, but I suppose there was no reason for it not to. We had prepared for it. We knew they would come eventually. It was only a matter of time. They had done it before, and there was every reason to believe they would do it again, especially with the French stirring up their emotions."

I sit rapt and silent as Mercy vigorously relates the story that she has wanted to tell me since I first told her about my affliction weeks ago. We have a moment now as we rest in the early morning, before taking on our chores.

"I remember that morning being especially cool and gloomy," Mercy says. "Otherwise, I do not remember anything after the raid had begun except for the relentless waves of native warriors."

I try to picture what Mercy is describing in my mind—the eastern frontier; the rugged coastline; the fierce, painted warriors on attack—but such things are difficult for me to imagine.

"They overwhelmed any opportunity we might have had to defend ourselves," Mercy says. "There seemed to be an infinite number of them—angry and out for blood. There was not an ounce of pity to be found in them. And they were not only pursuing the men. The women and children were also struck down without the slightest concern. Some of the warriors had guns—surely the French must have supplied them—but most of them beat us with their sticks or hacked away at us with their hatchets."

Such a terrible scene is unimaginable to me.

"It was raw vengeance, Anna. I saw more than a few men with looks of pure terror on their faces, running for their lives. I saw them cut down with a well-thrown hatchet or a powerful swing of a staff. It was worse than any nightmare, worse than anything even the most troubled mind could conjure up."

Despite my terror, I am insatiable for more.

"It could not have been more than a quarter of an hour into the melee, but it seemed like a lifetime to me. I had no idea what to do, and there was nobody to guide me to safety. Not a single person. All I could do was run. I suppose that is what one usually does when they are in such peril. It was the only thought in my mind: run."

"Where did you go?" I ask with urgency.

"I ran as fast as I could away from the fighting until I came upon a fur trapper's hut. I realize now how fortuitous it was that the hut was there—perhaps the Almighty had a hand in placing it there for my benefit. I hid there to get away from the fight, to get clear of the fort. I knew there was no chance we would be rescued this time."

"I am so afraid for you, Mercy," I say.

"I was afraid, too. Even when I was very young, I knew there were many who thought it unwise for us to be on the frontier. I even questioned Mother about it myself. 'It is our home, Mercy,' she would tell me. 'It is all we know. Why would we leave our home when it is all we have in this world?'"

"Your mother and father were not afraid to be there?"

"Not in the least. It seemed to be their destiny. When we came to Salem, after the first attack, I thought we would finally be safe, but I could feel it, Anna. I could feel something unsettling here, perhaps more unsettling than Maine. I think that is why I did not mind going back to the frontier, even with its dangers stalking us like a wolf."

"What was unsettling?" I ask, surprised to hear her say such a thing.

"I cannot be sure what it was about Salem," she replies. "It was just a feeling that I could not ignore. But mostly I missed my home. Like Mother said, it was our home, and I missed it. I missed the freshness of the mornings, the sense of purpose we carried with us. We were making the land into something, together, just as the Lord had intended us to do. And nobody should ever claim that life is meant to be easy. God has never promised us a simple path."

"Of course," I reply.

"As I cowered in that trapper's hut," Mercy continues, "I knew my parents were gone. How could they not be killed with so many warriors on the attack? I hope you will not think poorly of me, Anna. I loved my parents so very much, and I miss them so terribly now. It is frightful to think of how they must have met their end, the indignity of their deaths at the hands of some painted savage. Yet I was thinking mostly about myself in that moment. I suppose that makes me terrible, but I could not help but wonder what would happen to me. I suppose one never knows what one will think about in such situations until it is happening."

"I do not think poorly of you, Mercy," I reassure her. "I have had similar feelings. I have wondered myself what will become of me when my mother . . ." I trail off before completing my thoughts, but Mercy seems to take my meaning, accepting it with a solemn nod.

"I must have been in that trapper's hut for less than an hour when I heard him," Mercy continues. "At first, I thought he might be a warrior coming to finish me off. I was so frightened that I thought I would die. I was trembling with fear, cowering in a corner, praying for my salvation. Then I caught sight of this man and saw it was Reverend Burroughs. I could see him eyeing the hut, and I knew he would come in and see me hiding there."

"Reverend Burroughs!"

"Indeed, it was," Mercy responds. "I was not prepared for the look on his face when he laid his eyes upon me. Anna, it was as if the devil himself were inside of him. He had blood smeared upon his forehead, and his eyes were ablaze and wild with madness. I froze at the sight of him. There was a disquieting fire in his expression. He seemed to have a hunger within him."

"Oh dear, Mercy!"

"He said he was pleased to see me. It was such a strange utterance, given our circumstances. I suppose he was glad to know I was still alive, but it seemed an odd thing to say, nonetheless. He said he knew of a small boat we could take to the island in the bay where we could expect to be safe. He said we needed to hide in the hut just a little longer and wait for the attack to subside before we could make our move. He knew a way to go where we would not be detected by the warriors."

"Reverend Burroughs led you to safety?"

"That is not quite what happened," Mercy responds. "His appearance was not a relief to me in the least. In fact, I was quite unsettled at the thought of going anywhere with him. I did not want him to be my savior."

"I see," I reply. "But you had to go with him, did you not?"

"Of course. What else could I do? I hadn't any recourse other than to follow him on that wooded trail to the rowboat in the bay. Could I have told him I would not go with him?

Could I have said I would be fine on my own? I think about that every day, Anna. I think of how I could have said those things to him, gone away on my own and left him for good. I might have been killed, or I might have come to Salem and met you sooner. But I did not have the courage to do those things. My only choice was to go with the reverend. It did not matter how he had looked at me. It was the only thing that I could do. I hope you do not think poorly of me."

"Of course not, Mercy," I say. "I cannot imagine what you had to endure."

"We stayed on that little island in the bay for a few days," Mercy explains. "It was not easy but, in truth, he took good care of me. He foraged for berries and other things we could eat. He even found some fresh water for us to sip. While he was doing these things, while he was caring for me, I did not see that putrid look in his eyes. I did not see the devil living inside of him. But I know now that the devil is cleverer than to allow himself to be revealed when he does not wish to be seen."

"You are quite right," I respond. I know all too well the terrible things of which the devil is capable.

"I will never understand how he was able to usher us to that boat and row us out to that island in such safety," Mercy says. "We did not see a single warrior during our journey. Think of it. There had been thousands of them and now there were none. As the smoke from the burning fort began to subside, the reverend spoke to me about going back. Not for good, of course, but he wanted to go back to prepare for our journey to Wells, on the coast. It was where he said we had to go next, and he wanted us to go there together. He said we would be safe there."

"Why did the reverend think that you would be safe in Wells?"

"I cannot say for certain, because he did not tell me," Mercy replies. "But he seemed to think I belonged to him now, that he owned me, and I could not simply leave on my own and carry on as I saw fit. Of course, I would not have been capable of living on my own, even if I wanted to, but there was no question that the reverend wanted me to be with him. I was meant to be by his side. I was meant to serve him."

I could only manage a brief nod before Mercy continued.

"As I have told you, he was not unkind to me, not at first. Without him, I am not sure I would have had the courage to ever leave the trapper's hut in the first place. And I would have surely been found by some warrior who would have finished me off: hacked to me to death or taken me as a concubine. Reverend Burroughs was not tender or caring in the least. He does not seem capable of such feelings. But he took good care of me during our first days together, I cannot deny that."

I continue to sit silently listening, eager to hear more.

"When we arrived in Wells, everything changed," Mercy continues. "It was like the difference between night and day.

The look he wore when I first saw him in the trapper's hut returned. I do not know why he chose to take us to Wells. He seemed to think he could find work there as a pastor, or maybe it was some scheme in which he wished to involve himself. Any kindness he had shown to me during those days after the attack had disappeared entirely. He kept me mostly confined to a room with a tiny bed and the smallest of windows. There was barely any light shining through, but I cannot say it was a poor situation. I came to appreciate this small space—the whiteness of its walls, the strange shape of the windowpanes, the squeaking of the floorboards. It was my own and I was glad for it."

"He kept you in a room?"

"Yes. And he would come to me at all hours, but most often late at night. Sometimes he just sat with me on a small stool he would bring with him. He seemed to relish speaking to me. He did not even care if I responded to his words." Mercy pauses in thought for a moment before beginning again. "I am sure he was lonely," she says. "His wife had passed away not long before, and he seemed to have no acquaintances at all in Wells. We were both entirely alone there. But we never discussed these things. Instead, he would speak to me as if I were his property. He seemed to enjoy speaking to me in a degrading manner. He seemed to derive pleasure from treating me like a dog."

Mercy was becoming more emotional as she spoke, and I placed my hand on her arm to offer her what little comfort I could.

"I could see it on his face, Anna," Mercy continues, fighting tears, "that look in his eyes, the one he wore when he first found me in the trapper's hut. There was a wicked gleam to it. It was the look of a man possessed, the look of a man who is not entirely in control of himself."

"What did you do?"

"I did not engage with him at all during his nightly visits. I let him conduct them as he desired without the slightest protest or reaction. I knew that allowing him to continue unfettered would make it all the easier for me to endure. In truth, I did not understand very much of what the reverend spoke to me about. His discussions would twist and turn in strange and unusual ways."

"What would he say to you?" I ask.

"He would speak mostly about his power," Mercy says. "He was careful not to tell me whence it derived, but he would speak of it often. He would sometimes call me his queen. He spoke once about carrying me to the greatest heights and giving me anything I could manifest within my consciousness. His eyes would sparkle as he spoke wistfully about giving me whatever it was in the world that I wished to have, no matter how fanciful it seemed. But you must believe me when I tell you, Anna, I did not encourage such musings from him."

"Of course, Mercy! I believe you."

"I will never understand why he allowed such a thing, but one day the reverend told me that I should write to my sister in Salem. I did so as soon as I could obtain the paper and ink, and upon receiving my letter, my sister summoned me immediately. She told me about your family and how you needed a maidservant."

"I am so grateful for that, Mercy," I say. "But why did the reverend allow you to write to your sister?"

"I have no idea, but the reverend had no choice but to let me go once my sister had summoned me here. I am certain that is not what he had expected her to do, but he had no claim on me, and he knew it would be improper for him to make one. He could not afford to be ruined, so he had to let me go."

"It must have been God's work," I say.

"Perhaps. Yet it is strange how often he would speak about his immense power and riches, yet, all the while, struggle to scrape together whatever bits of gold and silver he could get his hands on. It seems it was all a charade."

"He is not a good man, Mercy."

"That is why I have told you this story. You must know that Reverend Burroughs is not a good man. You have done the right thing by accusing him. You should not doubt your instincts, my dear. Reverend Burroughs is no man of God. And I dare say he has never been such. I believe he is the very worst among us."

CHAPTER 16

They were identical wheels, sparkling like diamonds in the sun. It looked like they were wheels within wheels, like a gyroscope.

—Ezekiel 1:16

"It has been accomplished, Thomas," Edward tells me as I open the door. "I have just heard the news from Nathaniel that the magistrates are sending the marshals to arrest Burroughs. I came immediately to tell you."

"Praise God. We have done it!"

"What is it? Is that Edward?" I am surprised to hear my wife's voice from inside the house, inquiring about what is happening. I can tell from the vibrancy in her voice that she is particularly lucid.

"It is the letter that I have written to the magistrates, Ann—a letter about George Burroughs," I tell her.

"It has achieved its purpose," Edward adds, but he doesn't wait for her answer before he turns from our doorstep to head back to Ingersoll's for more news from the men at the tavern.

"Achieved its purpose?" Ann asks as she enters the room. "What purpose does Edward mean, Thomas? Tell me what has happened."

I am overjoyed by Ann's cogency. It is rare that we are able to converse in such a manner, and I am eager to take advantage of this opportunity.

"They have arrested Burroughs, my dear," I tell her, my voice enthusiastic. "I had known that the magistrates, Hathorne and Corwin, would require some additional convincing when it came to our complaint against Burroughs—"

"Oh, he is the worst of them!" Ann interjects.

"Indeed, my dear. But because he is our former pastor, I knew the magistrates would be ill at ease charging him without having some extra incentive. So I wrote a letter to supplement the complaint, explaining why he should be charged and brought in for examination. I wanted the magistrates to understand why we have made these accusations against him."

"You are so wise!" There is a glowing smile on Ann's face that makes her appear as she did when she was much younger, when she was unencumbered by her heavy burdens.

"You are too kind, my dear. I knew my letter needed to do more than simply inform them of Burroughs's evil dealings.

It needed to reassure the magistrates. Burroughs has hidden behind God for protection before, and I knew he would try to appeal to the magistrates as a humble servant of God."

"It would be a monstrous irony if George Burroughs's status as a member of the clergy were to protect his status as a minion of the underworld."

I am surprised by Ann's wise rejoinder, raising my eyebrows as she delivers it. "You are quite right," I say. "That was precisely my fear. We know what Burroughs is capable of. That is why my letter to the magistrates had to be unimpeachable."

"And so it appears that it has been," Ann says, then adds, "Thank God for that!"

As we stand together before the hearth looking into each other's eyes, we hardly know what to say. We both seem to be overwhelmed by the moment.

"How did you know that it would work?" Ann finally asks. "How did you know to write such a letter?" Her voice has a deliberate tone and her eyes seem to be probing my face for an answer.

"It was my intuition, I suppose," I respond. "I suppose that I understand men like Hathorne and Corwin. I have known men like them all my life. I understand that they require such reassurances. They expect to hear from leaders who can confidently tell them that the people of Salem are not some collection of simple-minded bumpkins who are spinning tales."

"I am grateful for your sound judgment," Ann says. "We should all be grateful for it."

"I simply wanted the magistrates to know the truth. They needed to understand that our community is ailing and that we are rightfully seeking justice to be dispensed through their wisdom and action." After a brief pause, I gingerly probe more, hoping Ann might be capable of pushing our conversation further. "I hope you do not think it arrogant of me to say that I am proud of what I have accomplished, my dear wife. I am eternally grateful to be able to share this great news with you. I thank God for what he has bestowed upon us."

As I look at Ann, standing before me in an attentive and animated posture, my emotions seem to bubble to the surface, and I struggle to contain them. God is smiling upon us, I believe. He has given Ann the strength and ability to understand this important news, and it has renewed my sense of purpose when I need it most.

"It is never arrogant to be truthful, Thomas," Ann says in a kind and thoughtful tone. She adds a tentative request: "Would you be so kind as to tell me what you have written to the magistrates, my dearest husband? I would like nothing more than to hear your wise words in my ear."

I am enormously pleased to carry out her request. The prospect of continuing our interaction in this manner fills me with energy. I eagerly lead my wife to her chair and sit down beside her.

Having worked on the letter for many hours, I have committed much of it to memory.

"As I have said, Ann, I am well aware of men like Hathorne and Corwin. I recognize that praise is the most expedient means for capturing their hearts. Such men are brittle, and must be reassured of their greatness with some regularity. So that is how I began my letter to these men."

I lean close to my wife's ear and whisper the first sentence in a slow and deliberate cadence, carefully enunciating each word: "After most humble and hearty thanks presented to your honors for the great care and pains you have already taken for us, for which we are never able to make you recompense..."

Ann responds with a deep breath and the slightest smile blooming on her lips. She settles further into her chair, trying to relax as she prepares herself to hear more.

"We thought it our duty to inform your honors of what we conceive you have not heard, which are high and dreadful: of a wheel within a wheel, at which our ears do tingle..."

"A wheel within a wheel," Ann says in a whisper to herself. "So clever, Thomas." Her eyes have closed and there is a slight edge to her voice.

"Humbly craving continually your prayers and help in this distressed case, so praying almighty God continually prepare you, that you may be a terror to evil-doers and a praise to them that do well."

"My husband has done us a great service," Ann says, again seemingly to herself, with her eyes still closed and a broad, bright smile upon her lips. "A wheel within a wheel, at which our ears do tingle," she repeats again in her breathy whisper, clearly impressed at my clever turn of phrase. "It is a reference to Ezekiel, is it not?" she asks, much to my surprise.

"Yes, dear, you are quite right," I respond. "I wished to convey the complexities that we are facing in this difficult moment. Moreover, I wished to let them know that I am a learned man too. It is important for them to understand whom they are dealing with."

"And you are quite a force to deal with, my husband. You are not some bumpkin seeing ghosts, are you?" she asks with a slight chortle.

"It seems that the devil could not save George Burroughs. Now he must answer for his devious actions before us and before God."

"His soul has been mortally wounded," Ann says in a knowing tone as she opens her eyes again.

"Please understand, my dear Ann, that it was Reverend Burroughs who did this to us. If you take nothing else from our presence, this is what you must remember. He is capable of the most vile and cruel behavior."

The two women are floating before me, tender and delicate. They are like a pair of angels sent from heaven. They stand close to each other, overlapping in a way that makes them appear almost as if they are one individual, shrouded in a translucent whiteness. Although I cannot tell what the material is made of, their shroud glows brightly. Even in the darkness of my room, it shines as blindingly as fresh snow on a sunny morning. Their bodies are entirely covered in their wrapping, from head to toe. Only their pale faces are visible to me beneath their shrouds. The brightness makes it difficult to look at them directly. Instead, I focus my eyes on their uncovered faces in order to hold my gaze, forced to squint my eyes to battle the glare.

I cannot place them, but their faces are familiar. They are not pretty, exactly, but they are not unattractive, either. They are plain and sturdy women, radiating warmth.

"We have not come to harm you, my dear. We do not wish to frighten you or to cause you any pain. We have come to you because you can help us, Ann. You are the one we have been waiting for."

Their pleasant and comforting smiles remain intact upon their faces as I hear their words inside my consciousness. I cannot tell if they are speaking to me directly or if I am able to understand what they wish to convey to me, but their words are reassuring. Their kindness and concern feel like blessings to me.

The specter of Reverend Burroughs and the Black Man are frolicking nearby, on the other side of my room. Yet in the presence of these women, they appear small and insignificant. The women, the specter of Reverend Burroughs, and the Black Man seem to be ignoring one another. Yet nothing will break my focus from the faces of these gentle and kind women.

Despite their outward smiles, the women appear to be harboring a deep sadness. It is as if they are in mourning. Yet, in spite of their melancholy, they continue to radiate a sense of deep and fulfilling warmth onto me. They seem comforted by my presence, relieved to be with me. I want nothing more than to be worthy of them.

"We are the wives of Reverend Burroughs," they tell me.

Although I am aware that the reverend has had wives before, I have never known who they were.

"It is important for you to understand that the reverend is responsible, Ann. It was he and only he who did this to us. It does not matter what he tells you. We want you to understand the truth. He is guilty of these crimes. Reverend Burroughs is a liar."

"I can hear you," I respond to the women, despite it being my usual custom not to interact with the specters I see. "I hope you know that I can hear you."

I am desperate for the women to hear me and to know I understand what they are conveying to me. Yet their expression does not change in response to my words. Their warm smiles remain in place, and they do not express the slightest anger or passion as they convey their story to me. Their deep compassion overwhelms me. I am not prepared to experience such tenderness, and as I do, tears begin to roll down my cheeks. Their grace seems to be too much for me to bear. And when they see my tears flow, they offer a sympathetic smile.

"We do not wish to cause you pain, my dear," they tell me. "Our only wish is for you to know the truth because that is what you need now, Ann. That is what will save you."

"God bless you," I utter reflexively.

"And may God bless you as well, my dear."

The woman on the right begins to delicately push aside her white wrappings to expose part of her left arm. I can see what appears to be a wax sealant, with a grayish hue to it, covering a portion of her skin. The other woman does not look at her companion's arm. Instead, her solemn expression remains fixed upon me.

The woman with the wax sealant begins to carefully peel the covering to reveal a large, gaping wound underneath that stretches from the top of her shoulder to nearly her elbow. As she does this, her face remains focused on mine, its warmth still radiating brightly toward me. She needlessly gestures, without looking, to call my attention to the unusually large opening in her upper arm—a jagged chasm with flaps of skin pushed in toward its darkness. Despite the gruesomeness of her injury, there is no trace of blood on the woman's bright pale skin.

"The reverend is responsible for this grisly wound, Ann. I am sorry to have to show it to you, but I want you to see for yourself what he has done to me. I want you to know that it was he who accomplished this grievous injury. He was in a blind rage one evening when he set upon me with a knife, thrusting it into my arm many times with a deep malice."

I shudder as I imagine the pain this woman must have endured as a result of the reverend's malevolence.

"I am very sorry," I say. "He is not worthy of you!"

"Bless you, my dear. Your compassion is admirable."

"I too have suffered much at the hands of the reverend," says the wounded woman's companion. She is not wearing a similar bandage or wax covering, like the other woman, but she makes it clear to me that she, too, is a victim of Reverend Burroughs's cruelty.

"Though my pain and suffering are not as visible, I too have suffered at the hands of the reverend. As his wife, he planned my death for years and took great pains to ensure that it was carried out in a most horrifying manner, slowly poisoning me with inheritance powder until I was incapacitated and brought home to God."

I am grateful that they have entrusted me with this information and I do my best to let them know my feelings.

"You will receive justice for your pain," I tell them. "I will avenge your horrible deaths."

"God has his own plans for George Burroughs, but justice cannot happen without your help. The magistrates must know what the reverend has done to us, but you cannot tell them what we have told you now."

"I do not understand. Why can I not tell them?" I ask.

"Because they will not believe that you have been visited by us from beyond the grave. You are well aware of our traditions, my dear. The living do not believe in such things. They will think you are mad. You must be clever, Ann. We know that you are clever."

I nod solemnly as the women begin to slowly recede into the background. As they fade away, a profound and intense sadness fills the void they are leaving behind. Once the women have fully disappeared, the darkness overwhelms me, and my tears return. I am crying uncontrollably as the specter of Reverend Burroughs and the Black Man, full-sized once again, begin to dance around me, taunting me with their ridicule in my grief. Their chortles grow louder and their dancing more intense as they sense my growing pain.

CHAPTER 17

When I first arrived, I found this province miserably harassed with a most Horrible witchcraft.
—**Governor William Phips**

MAY 30, 1692

Dear Edward,

You know as well as anybody that it is difficult for a man to admit when he is wrong. I believe most of us would rather knowingly continue with some foolhardy venture, all the while falsely declaring that we are correct, than be forced to admit our own folly. I fully accept that I am like most men in this regard, and I am sorry to have to tell you, my dear brother, that you are like most men as well. I suppose our positions within this community compel us to possess such certitude. Even the slightest wavering can bring about the most damaging of consequences.

You know that I have been sound in my own beliefs regarding Burroughs. He is among the most wretched of men. You are also aware that there have been whispers about him for years, swarming around him like locusts since his arrival in Salem. We should have listened to our hearts, my dear brother, and done what we knew to be God's will. Burroughs's piety was always a mirage. He is a charlatan, yet too many of us were thoroughly taken in by his cunningness. If our current troubles have taught us anything, Edward, it is that evil lives where we least expect it to. I know it is a frightening thought, but when I think of what has happened to my dear daughter, I cannot help but think about how insidious the evil that we are fighting is. We must be ruthless in our pursuit, Edward. It is our only hope of defeating such a beast.

Thank you for sharing the news of Sarah Osborne's death in jail. She was a weak and feeble woman, and I am not surprised by her demise under the harsh conditions. We know God was not on her side, but He saw fit to take her now, before earthly justice had been dispensed. I will not question why the Lord has chosen to take Osborne now, but her easy death does not sit well with me. I am grateful she is gone. Yet I longed to see her made an example. I wished to see her brought to justice for her sinfulness and cruelty against Anna and the other girls. I would have appreciated witnessing the very moment at her execution when her smug expression was wiped away by her fate. But we can be certain that she is in a far more difficult predicament now, Edward. You know as well as anybody that the Almighty's wrath is merciless upon such wretches.

I am heartened by our progress, Edward. The worst seems to be behind us now. The accusations and arrests are being conducted. God took care of Osborne, but the magistrates will soon dispatch Burroughs and the others. This is what swift and decisive action can accomplish, my brother. If there had been even the slightest hint of hesitation, we would not be enjoying this success.

Anna does not tell me as much as she once did. She is not well, and her silence requires me to probe deeper for the information that she once readily supplied. She walks about as if in a daze now. It has become difficult to know when she is experiencing her more lucid moments. Her visions seem to come at all times of the day and night. I am not aware of everything that she sees, but I know enough to act when it is required of me. I have written much of her testimony, Edward, but it is only to ease her burden. It seems we have opened the floodgates at last, and this evil is flowing out into the open where it can be more easily stamped out. Rumors that have been hidden away for years about Osborne and Burroughs, and others are no longer able to be obscured from us. The truth is finally being exposed.

I am proud of my daughter's fearlessness, Edward. I suppose I should have been aware that she possessed such fortitude and strength. You know her faith has always been strong—certainly, stronger than most. I always knew she would not hesitate to do what was necessary of her, but she has proven selfless beyond measure. I suppose we all must pay a price for goodness, Edward. She is handling her obligation with great nobleness.

I believe my daughter will soon be relieved of this affliction and will break free from its chains as we cast this evil asunder. Anna has already brought many of these wretches to justice with her bravery and strength. God will surely spare her soon from her sufferings. She is a Putnam, and you know that our strength is limitless in the face of need. She might just be the very best of us, Edward.

Surely you have heard by now the news of our new governor's arrival. Do you know that Sir William was born and raised on the eastern frontier, of all places? He is the first among us to be knighted by the king. It is strange to imagine how far this man has come—from the wilds of the heathen frontier to the gilded courts of London. Such a journey hardly seems possible. The governor and Reverend Mather are bringing the new charter home now. Dare I say that our situation is reaching a placid resolution? Time will tell, I suppose, but I am more sanguine than I have been in some time.

Have you heard the talk about the special court? They are calling it "Oyer and Terminer" ("to hear and to decide," my learned brother). It is to sit here in Salem and be presided over by Chief Justice Stoughton. I am impressed by this swift and decisive action. It bodes well for us, and I am anxious to hear what further details you might know. I pray that such encouraging developments might hasten our speedy recovery and usher in a new birth for our blessed City on the Hill.

I can imagine the smile on your face as you read these words, Edward. It brings me much comfort and pleasure to picture you in my mind. You know I have a weakness for grandiosity, but I know that you and the Almighty will forgive me in this case.

Brighter days are ahead of us, dear brother, I can assure you.

As ever, your most obedient servant,
Thomas

The heat under my skin is unbearable. It feels as though it is bubbling up from somewhere deep inside of me, generated within the depths of my soul. It is a raging inferno of hellfire, stoked for the sole purpose of causing me pain and misery. My condition is only getting worse now. There are times

when the fire is so hot that I must do everything in my power to avoid tearing wildly at my arms and legs, ripping away my flesh to expose whatever seems to be setting me alight.

Yet I know that doing so will not provide me with any relief. It will not reveal the culprit of my maladies, even if I somehow believe it might.

It is a constant and miserable pain. But perhaps pain is what I require more than anything else now. Perhaps pain is precisely what I need.

PART 2

Justice

CHAPTER 18

I am as innocent as the child unborn.
—**Bridget Bishop**

"You will keep silent," she said.

Bridget Bishop's words still haunt me days after she uttered them upon the gallows. What thoughts might she have been harboring in her mind as she stood there, stark and still, with the noose around her neck? What was running through her consciousness as her last breath was about to leave her body? Why does her simple phrase fester inside of me? Was she speaking of some unholy secret, or was it something else, something too wicked for us to know? As her body writhed on the rope, her words consumed me.

"You will keep silent."

Bishop claimed not to be a witch many times during her trial, yet not a single soul in this village believed her to be innocent of the charges. Despite her insistence, we were all convinced of her wickedness. Many of us were certain of it long ago.

I was an acquaintance of Bishop's deceased husband, Thomas Oliver, God rest his soul. He related to me while he was alive that his wife would sit up in bed at night muttering to the devil in some strange tongue. I can still see old Oliver's face, creased with fear, as he related this shocking news in a hushed whisper at Ingersoll's some years ago. He had tears in his eyes as he explained in vivid detail how his wife delighted in her discussions with Satan. He described how she would converse with the devil in the dark of the night, her eyes infused with a strange energy as she spoke in their unusual language. That poor man was deathly afraid of his own wife. He confided that he knew she had manifested some curse upon him. He believed then that he was not long for this world and, indeed, he died shortly after relaying this news.

Bishop was accused of murder by witchcraft upon her husband's death, but the charges were dismissed. It has now been more than a decade since Oliver's passing, but Bishop's current trial has properly renewed our interest in those events. How could it be possible for anyone to believe in this woman's innocence?

It was said that Bishop enjoyed junketing. Even as an old woman, she could be found frolicking about in search of carnal delights. She embraced all manners of pleasure without shame, not just those of the flesh. She often wore gaudy outfits—a red paragon bodice bordered with an array of vibrant colors, among other flamboyant garments. Yet we always held our tongues despite our knowledge about her. We were cowards for allowing such wicked behavior to continue unabated without so much as a cross word against it. Thrice married and entirely unworthy of the title "goodwife," we continuously looked the other way at her evil doings. But those days are over now.

We should be rejoicing at her demise, not questioning it, as Judge Saltonstall seems to be doing now. He is a weak man who lacks the constitution required for his work. It was not an easy death, I will grant that. Bishop swung violently upon the rope longer than any of us had expected her to. Yet in the end, the deed was rightfully accomplished, as God and the court had ordered it to be done. What dangers have we now prevented because of this sentence? Who among us knows what a witch is truly capable of?

It was plain upon her face the relish that she took in uttering that final haunting phrase, the last words of a cruel and calculating woman—whatever she meant by them. "You will keep silent," Bishop said as the hangman dispatched his duties.

I am glad she is dead. I rejoice in her demise.

I did not appear at Proctor's Ledge for Bridget Bishop's execution. I could not bear the thought of seeing her again, even if it was to witness justice being carried out. Father told me that she maintained her innocence to the very end–even as the executioner was placing the noose around her neck.

I had retired to my room the night before her execution with the knowledge that Goody Bishop's sentence would be carried out the following morning, hoping it might ease my burdens in some manner. Yet as I dozed fitfully in my bed, I felt more uneasiness than ever before. My stomach turned and my mind raced.

There have always been whispers about Goodwife Bishop, and I could not help but think of them as I lay restlessly in my bed. Even at a tender age, I was aware of her soiled reputation: quarreling, debauchery, thievery. She was once made to stand in the square as punishment for fighting with her husband on the Sabbath. I remember seeing her there when I was a young child, Mother quickening my step so I would not linger too long beside her. Goody Bishop wore a crudely written sign around her neck announcing the details of her crime–quarreled on the Sabbath, it read in uneven letters–as a cold drizzle pelted her from the heavens. I can never forget the look in her eyes as she stood soaking in the mud and rain. Her dark and dull eyes seemed to pierce me like sharp pins and follow me relentlessly as I made my way home.

It was that same figure, more weathered by age, who stood before me in my room. I had prayed mightily that Goody Bishop would spare me on the eve of her execution, but I knew in my heart I would see her again. I was certain of it.

"You say I believe that my God is the devil," her specter said in a low and smooth tone that chilled me to the bone. "You say I believe that the devil is our one true God, Ann. I know not what a witch is, but I know for certain about the devil. And you are playing with fire, my dear."

I did not respond to Goody Bishop's pronouncements, vowing to hold my tongue in the hope that she would leave me in peace.

"You say that I am a witch," she said in a firm and cruel voice. "You and your friends have accused me of this, and the court has believed your accusations. But tell me Ann, what is a witch?"

I remained silent.

"Is it a woman who chooses to live her life? A woman who enjoys the pleasures of the flesh or wearing fine clothing? A woman who wishes nothing more than to feel her existence as she lives it? Is that what my crime is?"

I continued my silence at Goody Bishop's queries.

"I did not utter a single word in my defense before that so-called court, Ann," the specter said. "Did you notice that, or were you too busy with your lies? While you and Abigail and Mercy and the others were putting on your performance, caterwauling at every movement of my head or every wave of my hands, I remained silent and dignified in court. Is that how a witch is supposed to act? You are liars! You know you are lying, and you must live with those lies forever!"

I continued my silence and vowed to remain so, come what may.

"The devil had a hand in my conviction," the specter said in a calmer voice. "You have brought the devil to this village, Ann. He has been hard at work here for many years, methodically whittling away at his weapons, sharpening them for battle, and you have helped unleash him. It will not matter for me. I will be finished now, but you will feel the full fury of his wrath." Goody Bishop's eyes narrowed and focused more intently upon me, piercing me with their sharpness. "It is your god that is the devil, Ann, not mine. It is you who has brought the evil hand upon us, not I."

I closed my eyes tightly, no longer capable of witnessing the intensity that Goodwife Bishop wore upon her face.

"You will pay a terrible price for what you have done, Ann," the specter said, before mercifully fading into the night.

CHAPTER 19

The wicked flee when no one pursues, but the righteous are bold as a lion.

—Proverbs 28:1

Nathaniel Saltonstall is a coward, and I am glad he has left the court. He was the weakest of them all, and as soon as I learned that he was appointed, I knew we would have trouble with him. I was as certain of it as I am that the sun will rise in the east tomorrow. He has no stomach for this business. The governor made a colossal folly by placing this man within the court's ranks, purely because of his wealth.

I have known Nathaniel Saltonstall since my service in the militia. Though I did not serve under the man, he had a well-earned reputation of being a uniquely ill-suited leader. The men would tease him behind his back about his smart uniform, with its brass polished up to a shine, but he is as spineless as any man I have ever known. His worst characteristic is his crippling indecisiveness. As any good military man knows, such a quality in a leader poses a grave danger to those in his command. Saltonstall sways like a reed shaken about by the wind, vacillating on every decision that comes before him. When he was an officer, his men would scurry about, urgently calling out orders that he refused to give, forced to manage the very responsibilities that had been entrusted to him while he sat like a dead tree stump, paralyzed by fear.

Why must we be so deferential to those with means? Saltonstall is the finest example of such foolish thinking. The weakness of this man's mind, body, and spirit are without question. He has no business being on a field of battle or in such a hallowed court of law as ours. As an officer, when he was not wavering about his command, he was yielding to the heathens at every turn, always quick to provide them with comforts and safety they had not earned. He seems to hold fast to the false belief that benevolence toward the natives will somehow compel them to transcend their wicked nature. I do not know if it is ignorance or cowardice—perhaps it is both—but Saltonstall's trepidation is an embarrassment to the righteousness of our cause. In the militia, his men eventually grew concerned about his incompetence and incessant anguish. I am surprised one of them did not put an end to their concern with a well-placed bullet. I suppose Saltonstall has their Christian charity to thank for his life.

To be sure, it serves our purpose that Saltonstall has left the court. Good riddance. I suspect that few now will listen to his concerns about the conviction of Bridget Bishop. She hasn't a friend remaining in this village and the court's work is quickly restoring order here.

Despite what Saltonstall may think, it is not possible to conjure up a more obvious witch than Bishop. She was provided with an abundance of Christian charity and mercy for the entirety of her long and wretched life, yet what did she offer us in return? Nothing but fistfuls of disdain and sinfulness. The old woman was properly judged, both here on Earth and now, surely, by the Almighty. The court had no choice but to condemn her for her many aberrant actions.

What would old Nathaniel Saltonstall have done differently? Slap Bishop on the wrist and hasten her efforts to corrupt our community further? The stakes are far too high for us to suffer such fools gladly now. That is what the devil wishes for us to do, and he will not hesitate to use our proclivity for Christian grace and forgiveness against us if we are not careful.

I wish Anna had been at Bishop's execution. I wanted her to witness the demise of the woman who has so ruthlessly tormented her. My poor daughter said she could not bear it. Alas, it was a disappointment for me; I had wanted us to revel in our victory together.

My world is on fire and burning out of control.

My tormentors celebrate my sufferings and exploit my weaknesses with much ease. I have no defenses against them, it seems. Even when I am not being haunted by them—during my fleetingly rare moments of tranquility—I am not fully awake to this world any longer. A haze has overcome me entirely. My mind is a swirl of jumbled thoughts and visions, a blanket of exhaustion that no amount of rest can uncover. I am reduced to little more than a dull and tedious entity.

My tormentors are meeting their fate at the gallows now. It has been but a few weeks, yet justice is being accomplished swiftly. The court has taken its oath as our protector seriously. Still, even the execution of my tormentors has not provided me with the faintest relief. It seems to have only stirred them up all the more, like the wind whipping up a dust cloud in the dry heat of summer. The specters descend upon me relentlessly now. Their pace seems to have quickened. Most of them are unknown to me. Even if I could make accusations against them, I would not know whom to accuse. Many do not even take human form but instead exist in the shape of strange animals or otherworldly beings.

My consciousness has been fully polluted. What the specters do in my presence no longer scares me as much as the residue of thoughts and images they leave behind when they go. These thoughts linger with me and twist themselves within my consciousness. The specters know exactly how to induce my fear. They tell me I am no good and have never been so. They say that my so-called Lord has rejected me. They tell me I will not join Him in the Kingdom of Heaven. They say that my lack of love for my mother is the reason for her doomed condition and that she knows this to be the case as well. They tell me she blames me for her troubles. I am the reason she has had to endure so much.

They tell me Mother has signed the devil's book, if only to get relief for herself. They tell me, too, that she will not receive an ounce of relief; she is damned to hellfire for all eternity. They explain how my betrayal of Abby and Betty through my disbelief in their fortune-telling was what unleashed this hell upon us. I opened Pandora's box and set this fury alight against my own people. I have angered Satan and caused him to attack us in this gruesome manner.

They are cunning. I know they are trying to deceive me, but their words are impossible to ignore. I can muster no defense against their taunts and accusations. My most humble desire now is for rest, to enjoy the peaceful comforts of sleep and awaken in the warm embrace of my mother, with her gentle smile glowing down at me from above. I want to feel the safety of her arms around me. I want to savor her love, even if I know her condition will never make that possible for me again.

I know in my heart that Mother's love for me was palpable once, even if I cannot feel it now, even if I have not felt it for a long time. I know I have not invented this belief. Her love used to wash over me like a waterfall. I would bathe in its warm and comforting flow. I will not allow them to take that knowledge away from me.

I have always loved my mother, and my love for her will always remain. I find myself speaking to her at random moments in the dark, as if she can hear me: *Do you know that it was I who stroked your hair and mopped your brow when you needed comfort, Mother? I would stay awake at night to soothe you when Father was not capable of doing it, too worn down by his own burdens. I was the one who gave you what you needed when nobody else could bear it, Mother.*

Your screams and cries have always been unsettling to me. Still, I believe you do not mean the things you have said to me. I know you do not wish that I was never born—that none of us had ever been born—and that you would like to run away from us, that you would like to flee to the frontier, never to return. I know these are not your true feelings, my dearest mother. It is your troubles that prompt you to say such things. I am aware of your love for me, even if you do not know it. Oh, please hear me, Mother, I say. *I pray you can hear what I am telling you, that you will know in your heart that what I am saying is true.*

CHAPTER 20

That there is a devil is a thing doubted by none but such as are under the influence of the devil. For any to deny the being of a devil must be from ignorance or profaneness worse than diabolical.

—Cotton Mather

My half-brother Joseph was at Ingersoll's ordinary during those first examinations on that stormy spring day. When I walked into the tavern, drenched from head to toe by that unrelenting downpour, I was surprised to see his face. My spirits were even lifted by the sight of him, which is hardly my typical reaction to Joseph. I suppose I might have allowed myself a fleeting moment of indulgence to revel in the fantasy that he was present there to represent our family, as Edward and I were. Alas, I should have never allowed myself to entertain such a romantic notion. He has been a contrarian from the beginning, and that is what he will always be. It is how God has made him: a fighter who is prepared always to fight, regardless of the harm he inflicts upon others.

My father was already an old man when he was wedded to Mary. I cannot deny that I was disappointed in the match, but I also could not blame him for wanting it. Of course, there was nothing I could have done to stop the matter even if I had wished to. Mother had passed away a few years earlier, and my father was lonely and needed a companion with whom to live out his days. It is expected of any man, and it should not be denied to those who deserve it most, as my father did. Still, I cannot pretend I was pleased he had chosen her, though it could never be said that I was displeased with the contentment he found in her. I suppose I was pleased for my father's sake.

Mary was a Porter, but that meant very little to Father. He was much too secure in his own greatness to be concerned about such things. He did not seem capable of recognizing that there might be some greater meaning in these matters. Even if he were capable, it would have been of little concern for him. Father saw Mary as nothing more than a well-born, God-fearing woman who would take good care of him in his old age. She was a delightful nymph who unleashed limitless devotion upon him. Father consumed that devotion as if it were a feast.

When he expressed a desire for marriage, Mary acted as if she had been chosen for coronation—proud as a peacock.

Father would never have admitted it to anyone, but I believe he enjoyed Mary's ostentation. It seemed to give him a renewed energy, a burst of vigor for his final years on this Earth. It was an unexpected rebirth for an old man. Mary's enthusiasm and fidelity were gifts from the heavens. She was Aphrodite swooping down from Mount Olympus.

Mary's inexorable sunniness radiated over my father like a warm spring afternoon, but that ceaseless energy seemed also to make him numb to the surrounding world. It seemed to soak up all that was in its path and suffocate anything that attempted to penetrate it. Perhaps that was her intention. If I were a more cynical man, I might suggest that Mary knew exactly what she was doing with her marriage to my father, but it is not my place to make such accusations.

For my father, the fact that Mary was a member of the Porter family meant only that she was also of prosperous stock. That was all that mattered to him, and he did not give her heritage one thought more. The scheming and machinations of our modern world were lost on his antiquated soul. If such things were brought up in his presence, he would simply dismiss them. "Whispering is unbecoming," he would say with a furrowed brow and a wave of his hand. In truth, his existence was a simple one. It was small. He was a quaint relic of a long-forgotten past. And once Mary had ambled into his life, his world became smaller still.

Given the circumstances of their relationship, Mary easily convinced my father to have yet another child, and Joseph is the one God chose to give to them: my much younger, hot-tempered half-brother. Joseph is firmly ensconced in the current generation. He wishes for Salem to undergo a metamorphosis, and he is passionate about ensuring that it happens precisely in the way he prefers. I do not know him well, of course. I was already a man making my way in the world when he was born. Yet what I do know has provided me with little reassurance.

As soon as Joseph was born healthy, I knew Father would see to it that he got the lion's share of his property. I had resigned myself to this fate long before it became a reality at my father's death, some fifteen years later. Though I was prepared, I cannot deny it was still a painful blow. It landed like a punch to my stomach and produced a dull ache that lingered for some time. Regrettably, my years of devotion to my father had meant little to him in the end. Those day-long journeys into the forest—just the two of us—all those years ago; his tender and patient tutelage; the careful efforts he made to ensure I was equipped with the knowledge and the skill I required to be a leader in this world: None of it seemed to have any meaning in the end.

In time, my disappointment diminished. I convinced myself that Father believed I had already done well enough in the world. I was a man now who no longer required his assistance. The land he had given to me upon my marriage to Ann had served its purpose. I had become successful, so there was nothing more for him to do. It made good, rational sense, of course. Still, I could never entirely banish the thoughts about where my family might be had we inherited what was always meant to be ours. I have spent days at a time building castles in my mind, imagining what will never come to pass. I cannot deny how I have rued the fact that it was Joseph my father chose to empower. An impure, bastardized Putnam—a Putnam *and* a Porter—who could hardly count more than a few days of true labor to his name was the one who had robbed me of my family's hard-earned legacy.

I am convinced Father was entirely unaware of what he had done. He could not have realized what his actions would portend for our family. Yet, it is of no importance now. Joseph won. Besting my—our—great father, he is now a flint poised to ignite the gunpowder that could destroy all that we Putnams have built here for generations.

There are some here who believe I am favored by God. Nathaniel Ingersoll likes to joke with me about such things. He seems to assume my life has been a bounty of promise, an endless supply of sunshine and fragrant blossoms. It is a tidy and expedient narrative for some to believe. Yet that does not make it reality. I have fought far too many battles to count in my life, and I am not ashamed to say that I have lost a few of them.

To be sure, the past was a simpler time. It is a common refrain, I am aware, but it is no less true for being so. My father was a farmer, like his father before him. They established these bountiful holdings under the watchful and protective eye of the Almighty, and they wanted nothing more than to work hard, serve the Lord, and help their community thrive. They wanted to build something great for God and civilization. They did not earn their wealth to enjoy a bounty of individual pleasures. Instead, they used their wealth for the benefit of us all, and their altruistic efforts earned them much respect and appreciation.

Perhaps it was inevitable that they would earn resentment and jealousy for what they have accomplished. It is a peculiarity of our nature that God, in His infinite wisdom, infuses us with such a range of contradictory emotions. Father was not immune to animus. Yet, in his ignorance and innocence, he was not always aware of the dangers lurking around him. I have learned from his naiveté. I will not make the same mistakes he made. My eyes are open to the true nature of man.

Father is with me now, as he often is in the evenings, sitting by my bed. I am feeling the way I usually do now, as if a dense fog is hanging over me, obscuring my thoughts. I struggle to comprehend what is happening around me, but I am also unable to rest, trapped in a hellish netherworld. But Father is here, and I am aware of that much.

"You are strong, Anna," he tells me in a surprisingly soothing and soft voice. He is trying to nurture my strength. "It is nearly finished, my daughter. I promise it will be over soon."

I can see him through my blurred vision, framed within the twilight of the evening. He is tired and looks weak and small as he sits before me.

The Black Man is listening to us from the shadows. I can see his white teeth as he chortles at my father's kind words to me. He seems to be dismissing them as folly. The Black Man is always lurking and always laughing. He is always reveling in my distress.

"He is a liar, Anna."

I can hear these words clearly in my head. Is it the Black Man speaking to me? He has not spoken before.

"You will never escape the devil that you have unleashed here, Anna."

The voice continues, and I can see Sarah Wildes standing with the Black Man now. She has hurt me and Mercy and many others, and so she has been rightfully accused. She is on trial now before the court. Her sorcery is being exposed by her neighbors. She is sure to face the executioner.

"It is true, Anna," Goody Wildes tells me now. "I am a witch, as you say I am. Despite my denials to the court, I have been enriched by the powers invested in me by the devil for decades."

Father is unaware that Goody Wildes and the Black Man are here with us, and he continues to stroke my hair kindly and offer his soft words of encouragement.

"Your father is a weak and feckless man," Goody Wildes tells me with eagerness in her voice. "He has shut your poor mother away. He is ashamed of her. He wishes for her to die. He wishes she had run off to the frontier, as she always threatened to do."

As usual, I say nothing in response to Goody Wildes's revelations. Even if I wished to respond to them, I haven't the strength to do so.

"I have bewitched many in this community, Anna," she tells me. "But your father has not needed my sorcery to stumble. He has fettered away your family's once-great legacy with his incompetence and vanity." Goody Wildes glares disdainfully at Father with a crooked smile as she speaks. "Your mother is too good for him. He was her greatest folly. If your mother were here with us now, she would admit as much without the slightest hesitation. Your father has humiliated her, and she despises him for it."

The Black Man is now stifling a quiet laugh at Goody Wildes's words.

"I know your mother well, Anna," she continues, seemingly eager to reveal more. "She is among our great circle. There is great power in this circle."

It is not clear to me what Goody Wildes means by the term circle, but I am too weak to even offer an inquisitive look in response.

"He has created this great circle to help us gain control," she explains. "We are comrades, you see, and we work together for his benefit."

The Black Man seems to become more animated as Goody Wildes speaks.

"We have been empowered by our one true god," she tells me now. "We have been empowered by Satan himself."

Goody Wildes carefully draws out both syllables of the word Satan and then breaks into a wide, toothy grin. Meanwhile, at the sound of the word, the Black Man hops with excitement. My father, tired and entirely ignorant of what is happening around us, remains next to me on his chair, seemingly lost in his own thoughts and too weary to get up.

"Your mother is a witch," Goody Wildes tells me. "She gave herself to the devil long ago, just as I and the others have done. Her condition is a ruse, designed only to fool your ignorant father. He has been bewitched by her in the most devious manner."

My eyes widen at this revelation, but I remain silent. My father remains close by in his chair, weak and clearly unaware of his surroundings. The Black Man has made his way toward my father now, seemingly up to something.

"Your mother is of perfectly sound mind; you must understand this fact," Goody Wildes continues. "She is aware of everything she is doing. She is merely playing a role as a mad woman so that she can drag your wretched and cruel father into the mud."

The Black Man places his dark hands upon my father's shoulders, though Father seems to remain unaware of the Black Man's presence.

"It will destroy him eventually," Goody Wildes says. "Your mother's performance will one day weigh too heavily upon your father's shoulders and finish him off."

The Black Man is leaning heavily into my father now, pressing down hard upon shoulders with all his might. I notice a palpable discomfort upon my father's face.

"Your mother is among the most brilliant women in our circle," Goody Wildes tells me with a hint of admiration in her voice. "Your mother is far more clever at her bewitchings than most of us."

The Black Man wears a grimace as he strains to press down upon my father's shoulders with his full strength.

"It will not be long now," Goody Wildes continues. "Soon you will know when your mother's plans have come to fruition. The results will be obvious."

With a great sigh, I hear my father stand up from his chair beside my bed. In the same instant, the Black Man and Goodwife Wildes disappear.

"Get some rest, my daughter," Father says, seemingly into the ether, as if he assumes I am asleep. "I will see you in the morning."

CHAPTER 21

I speak as to sensible people; judge for yourselves what I say.

—1 Corinthians 10:15

Reverend Parris has come to my home again to pray for Anna and the others this evening, but we spend most of our time together in conversation rather than in prayer. There is far too much happening now, and we are compelled to discuss it. The reverend is tired. His well-worn face makes that clear for all to see. Still, he perseveres, as we all must.

"What is on your mind, Samuel?" I ask him as we settle into chairs by the hearth. "You know you can unburden yourself with me. Allow me to lighten your load."

"I appreciate these sessions more than you can understand," he responds. "I suppose the more appropriate question to ask might be what is *not* on my mind. I am afraid it is alight with a multitude of thoughts."

"You are not alone."

Reverend Parris leans toward me in his chair and surprises me with his sudden query. "What do you know of Mary Walcott?"

I am intrigued about what has piqued his interest in my niece. "Not as much as you might think, despite her relation to me," I reply truthfully. "She is still young. Eighteen, I believe. There is nothing unordinary about her, I suppose. Why do you ask?"

"She has been on my mind," he tells me. "She has been quite a prolific accuser."

"So has Anna, and so have many of the girls. Alas, there is much evil here—"

"Do you know why I sent Betty away?" Reverend Parris interjects. "Why it was that at the first instant of her affliction, she was sent off to stay with Captain Sewell?"

"I assume you wished to keep her safe," I respond. "To remove her from harm's way."

"I received a letter from Captain Sewell a week or so ago," Reverend Parris says. "He informed me that Betty is nearly herself now. She is hardly showing any signs of her previous affliction."

"Praise God! That is wonderful news. Perhaps there is hope for Anna, then, and for the others as well."

Reverend Parris offers no reaction to my response.

"Why have you asked about Mary, reverend?" I ask when he remains silent. "What does she have to do with Elizabeth's improvement?"

"My mind is a jumble," the reverend says with a deep sigh. "It is difficult for me to know which thoughts connect to the next. I have been thinking about the examination of Sarah Cloyce, from last spring."

"Rebecca Nurse's sister? Her examination was months ago. Why are you still thinking about such a thing?"

"There have been so many examinations," he says sharply, shaking his head. "So many accusations. So many examinations..."

"We are in the middle of a battle," I say. "We might be in the midst of a great war, for all we know."

"I am thinking about Goody Cloyce," the reverend says quickly before I can say more, "because Mary Walcott was present during her examination. I remember seeing her there as I was taking notes."

"Of course. Many of the afflicted girls appear at the examinations. You know it is helpful for them to be present during—"

"She was knitting, Thomas," Reverend Parris interjects. "While the other girls were writhing upon the floor of the meetinghouse, screaming at the tops of their voices, Mary Walcott sat as calmly as a millpond, engaged in her knitting."

I am unsure how to respond to this unusual revelation, but I try my best to offer something. "I am sorry, but I do not see how that is relevant to our situation."

My words seem to induce an awkward silence between the two of us, and we remain silent for a long moment. Reverend Parris seems to be turning over some thoughts in his mind as he stares at the fire. Finally, he responds, "Perhaps you are correct. Perhaps it does not matter what Mary Walcott was doing during the examination. I suppose God equips us to react to such things in our own way. But . . ." The reverend trails off, shaking his head slightly. He seems frustrated, perhaps by his inability to make sense of the thoughts swarming around within his consciousness.

"Samuel, we are dealing with an unprecedented matter here," I tell him, hoping to ease his concerns. "You are correct that each of us is dealing with this condition in the way God has equipped us to. You were correct to send Betty away, and she is all the better for it. Perhaps I should have done the same for Anna, but she has wished to continue living here as best she is able, and I have not had the heart to go against her wishes, the poor girl."

"Thomas," the reverend says, "I do not judge you for what you have chosen to do for Anna. Those are the affairs of your family, and you will always have my respect and support regardless of the course of action you choose. That is not any of my concern."

"What is it that troubles you then? Please unburden yourself to me. That is why we are friends."

"To be truthful, I do not know precisely what troubles me," he responds. "Only that I am unsettled. Perhaps that makes me a weak man."

"We are all unsettled by this business," I tell him. "There is no shame in how we are feeling."

"Thomas, I cannot help but feel God has been righteously spitting in my face for many years now."

I am taken aback by the reverend's crass statement and can think of no response to it before he continues speaking.

"Since I took over my father's thriving plantation in Barbados and lost it all, since I failed as a merchant in Boston, in spite of the money I had at my disposal . . ." Reverend Parris pauses for a moment. "And now this."

"God tests us," I say in a soft and steely voice, trying to focus the reverend's attention. "We are all tested by Him. It is our lot in life."

"I know I should believe what you are telling me," he replies. "Yet I will never understand why He has chosen to test me so relentlessly. What have I done to deserve such punishment?"

"It is not for us to question such things."

"Of course not." His tone is resigned; he seems to acknowledge his need to shake off this malaise. "I am grateful for your kindness and companionship, my friend."

The Lord to me a shepherd is,
want therefore shall not I:
He in the folds of tender grass,
doth cause me down to lie:
To waters calm me gently leads
restore my soul doth he:
He doth in paths of righteousness
for his name's sake lead me.

Mother's voice was beautiful then. I was far too young to understand the words she sang, but I can never forget her voice. Its crispness and tone seem to have been seared within my consciousness to remain there, unaffected by anything that has happened since. I cling to that bold and strong voice as a drowning person might cling to driftwood in the sea, holding on so that it might save me. Mother's voice carried her love in its song, and I embrace that love, still today.

I miss Mother. I miss her kindness. I miss her pleasant and reassuring smile, her firm and calming sense of certainty. I miss when she was strong, and I pine for her to show that strength again, because I need it now more than ever before. Yet I know it will not come back. It seems that anguish is all she is feeling now. Sometimes I can hear her cry out. Even in my fog, I hear her cries ring out through our home. She does not seem to be crying for mercy now. Her cries are angry, filled with venom. They are cries for retribution.

I can see that Father does not know what to do with her. He does not understand how to release her from her pain. He tells me she is well, that she is only tired or weighed down by the many burdens God has chosen to place upon her shoulders. He says I should be assured that her faith and her devotion and her piety will provide her with the strength to prevail. He tells me the Almighty is watching over her, always. He says these things with such certainty that I almost believe them. He says that we—my mother and I—will persevere and be whole again soon.

"We are Putnams," Father says to me with his chest swelling and his pride on full display. "We are meant to prevail. We are strong, and we will only get stronger."

I can see he believes his words, but I cannot tell if I should feel sorry for him because of it. How will I be strong again? How will mother be strong again? It is unimaginable.

The Black Man is lurking here again, walking lightly upon his toes. He thinks he is hiding from me. He thinks he is clever, but I can see him. I always see him, even when he surely must believe that I do not. He cannot hide from me. But is he trying to hide? Perhaps he realizes I understand his games well enough by now. Perhaps he is having his way with me. Is this but a game to him?

Perhaps Father is correct. Perhaps I will get stronger one day, just as he says I will. Only God knows for certain. I pray that the Lord will have mercy on me, even if the Black Man laughs at my silent prayers. Perhaps he is correct to find it humorous. I cannot see how God will answer my prayers now.

The Black Man does not speak to me, but he is laughing softly at my prayers. He finds humor in my suffering and in my prayers for mercy. Does he know my thoughts? His white teeth are showing. They match the bright whites of his eyes precisely. They shine brightly, even in the darkness. He is trying to hide his teeth from me now. Is he embarrassed? He cannot hide them, though. No matter how hard he tries, I can see his teeth so clearly. I can see them more clearly than I can see anything else. They are sharp and pointed. They are exactly as one would expect the devil's teeth to be.

The Black Man is crouching near my bed now. He is down low, near the floor. Sometimes he even crawls on his hands and knees toward my bed, with his head lowered down against the floor. Does he believe I cannot see him? It cannot be possible he would be so ignorant as to believe I do not know he is always with me.

The yellow bird is at my window now. Was she always there? I have come to welcome her visits, despite the pain she brings to me. She is singing her awful song. The Black Man seems to be enjoying the yellow bird's vile melody, encouraging her awful caterwaul with his wretched swaying. Is he mocking me? Is he ridiculing my pain? Is he reveling in it?

I clasp my ears tightly with my hands and close my eyes. It is my only defense against such misery. I have no other means of fighting this evil. I suddenly find myself moaning to drown out the dreadful noises the yellow bird is making. The sound has struck some dissonant chord within me, and I am convulsing sharply, losing control. My thoughts spin wildly, uncontrollably within my mind. I am made dizzy by this whirling nightmare and by the jarring sounds that are growing louder and more irritating, ringing like loud, heavy bells within my ears. The Black Man is dancing. He wishes only to make me feel worse. My mind is making a million calculations a second as the cacophony builds to a terrifying crescendo.

How will it end? That is all I can think now. "How will it end?" I utter the words aloud to nobody at all.

My mind can take no more, but I am powerless to stop the din. I feel like I am being driven to the edge of madness. I am on a high cliff, preparing to jump into a vast, airy abyss. I press my palms so hard against my ears that my skull begins to ache. My eyes are shut so tightly, my eyelids feel as though they will burst. I can do nothing to stop this misery as it grows more intense around me, enveloping me in a sea of suffering. I am engulfed within a terrifying tempest, inching ever closer to the edge of the cliff.

My feet are over its edge now—it is an impossibly high cliff with an endless darkness stretching out below. A stiff breeze is all it will take to break my tenuous hold and toss me over the edge. It is all I need to end this misery forever. Still, it continues unabated, pursuing me ceaselessly and without mercy. I can do nothing but endure it for as long as it goes on.

"I will prevail, Father," I whisper through the din. "I will prevail."

CHAPTER 22

Our doubts are traitors, and makes us lose the good we oft might win, by fearing to attempt.
—**William Shakespeare's**
Measure for Measure

I will never get used to the executions. It is unwise for any man to become accustomed to such a thing, regardless of the justice being dispensed as a result. Still, there should be no confusion about the fact that we are witnessing justice before our eyes.

The hangman has placed the noose around Sarah Good's neck now, and she is standing on the cart, only a few feet from ground. Her rightful death is so close. Reverend Noyes is here again. He seems to believe that as Reverend Parris's assistant, it is his grim responsibility to take on the thankless work of offering these condemned women their final opportunity at repentance. He is only doing his duty,

I suppose, but it is a fool's errand. Sarah Good's soul, like the others, will surely be damned.

As the reverend approaches the cart, Good is glaring at him menacingly, clearly prepared to reject any notion of repentance in her final moments.

"Do you repent against the actions of which you have been rightfully convicted, Goodwife Good?" the reverend asks in his thin and nervous voice. "Do you condemn witchcraft and pledge your soul to the Lord for all eternity?"

Sarah Good attempts to take a breath through the tight, thick rope that is restricting her air. Then, steadying herself as best she can upon her feet, she prepares to respond.

"I am no more a witch than you are a wizard," she says to Reverend Noyes in a growl, her voice scratchy and worn and her eyes ablaze with fire. "And if you take my life, God will give you blood to drink."

The poor, frightened reverend is clearly taken aback by Good's fiery response, seemingly at a loss as to what he should do next in the face of such venomous words. He remains standing awkwardly beside her as she towers over him from the cart. He appears shocked into silence and wears a wounded look upon his face. He will surely have nothing more to say to this condemned woman now.

After a few seconds of silence, the hangman seems to have seen enough and gets to work, further tightening the already snug rope, which has been slung over the mighty branch of a heavy oak tree, around Good's neck. Reverend Noyes slowly steps away, disappearing among the crowd with a look of embarrassment set firmly upon his face. As the hangman tends to his final preparations, Sarah Good's face contorts with discomfort, and she begins to struggle. Is this condemned woman attempting to somehow escape her fate before our eyes? It is of no consequence. The hangman's quick and firm hands upon Good's body and the tightening of the rope binding her hands behind her seems to put an end to her restlessness. Sarah Good's fate is sealed.

After a brief moment, the hangman receives a nod from Sheriff Corwin, which results in his own signal to the driver, who suddenly whips and calls out to his horse. Immediately upon receiving the whip, the horse neighs loudly and jerks forward in a sudden motion, pulling the cart out from underneath Sarah Good. The rope extends, and she drops to within a foot or two of the dusty and parched soil, her toes stretching tantalizingly close to the ground. Her breath seems to have left her body immediately after her fall from the cart, and she begins to convulse violently, stretching her feet wildly in some futile attempt to reach the soil below them.

We watch in silence as Good's struggles continue for several breathless moments. Her body rhythmically moves back and forth as if she is a snake. The only sound she has made was a muffled breath upon falling from the cart. Now she is silent, making only movements: back and forth, back and forth, back and forth.

When will it end? I am transfixed, as are we all, witnessing Sarah Good's descent into hell.

It seems to be a long time before her body finally stops moving. Yet, even then, the hangman knows enough not to cut her down too quickly. It is another ten minutes or so before Sarah Good's body is finally removed and placed into the cart.

Justice has been done.

As I drift off into a fitful slumber, induced by the heat, I am suddenly startled awake by a bright light and a piercingly dissonant sound. My cloudy mind attempts to focus on the cacophony. The heat grows more intense, singeing the tiny hairs upon my skin. The clouds begin to part within my consciousness, and I can make out the form of Reverend Burroughs standing before me.

His face is rearranged in the most hideous manner. His eyes are where his mouth should be, and his ears are where his eyes should have been. His mouth is in the middle of his face, about where a nose might be expected. His nose is nowhere to be found at all. Despite the deformity of his face, I am certain that it is the reverend. I can tell by his figure, which I have seen so many times standing over me from the pulpit of the meetinghouse.

The hair atop his head is alight with flame, and tiny streams of black smoke rise above it. His neck is red and marred by the deep and unmistakable scar of the noose. His large and growling mouth dominates his face. He has an unusual and dangerous energy about him that seems unrelenting and menacing.

His specter is alone. The Black Man and the others are not here. As Reverend Burroughs lurches in my direction, I can feel the heat from the flames atop his head scorch my skin. I am surprised by how hot they are, and I wonder for a fleeting moment if the fire has originated from hell itself.

"You have betrayed me, Anna," he says.

I do not respond.

"We made a pact, you and I," he continues in an angry voice. "You signed the devil's book, just as I have. You and I are the same. We are meant to accomplish great things together."

I do not recall having signed the devil's book. Despite my condition, I have made a great effort not to do so. Yet I say nothing in response. I am not certain that I would be able to speak, even if I wished to. My tongue is tied by fear.

"Do you understand that I cannot be killed?" he asks me in an irritated tone. "At least, I cannot be killed in the way that you mortals think of death. It does not matter what you feckless *hypocrites do to my earthly body; my spirit will continue to haunt those who have wronged me for all eternity."*

I am mesmerized as the reverend's anger builds further.

"The Indians tried to kill me, Anna," he continues. "They tried many times before on the eastern frontier. My servant girl, Mercy, told you our story, did she not? You know the truth about me. You understand that because of the power bestowed upon me by the underworld, I am impervious to attacks. The savages could do nothing to harm me. My resilience caused the natives to view me as their god. Imagine that! Your own reverend, a god upon Mount Olympus! Their reverence caused me to see them as my only true ally in this world. They are savages, certainly, but they are not our enemy, not in the least. Instead, we are fighting together against our real enemy, and it is an insidious evil. Our enemies are those who call themselves the children of God. It is they with whom we are at war. They are the ones who must be destroyed."

Reverend Burroughs is speaking in a slow and deliberate voice, as if I am a small child and he wishes to make certain he is being understood.

"Anna, I know that you also recognize Satan as the one true god. I am still a reverend, you know, and it is my mission to spread the true Word. You can see the bright light that is also visible to me, even when others reject it. You recognize how wrong these people have been. You know that ours is the only way forward. I have been enlightened, and I know that you have been enlightened as well. That is why I have come to you. We have learned the truth, you and I. We no longer believe the lies we have been told for so long. We have been set free by the truth, yet we know that they will not believe us. They do not like to be told that they are wrong. They would sooner plunge to their deaths off a steep cliff than be forced to admit that they must change course to survive."

Reverend Burroughs begins to plead with me now: "I know you understand me. You, of all the people in this wicked and cruel world, understand who I am and know that I am a good man. I am begging you to show me your grace and your mercy, as I have always shown to you.

"My prophecies have been ignored. Please, my dear Anna, you are my only hope now. You know I am correct and I have always been correct. You understand how wrong they are. They mean well, I know they do, but they have been misguided by generations of liars, directed by charlatans down a dark pathway. It is not their fault, but you know this is the truth. Take this journey with me, and together, we will turn the tide of history. You must join me. You cannot deny your destiny."

A gnawing sense of sympathy for the reverend begins to well up inside of me. I am surprised to feel such emotion for this man, but I seem to be powerless to stop it. Perhaps I am a victim of his trickery. Perhaps this is the reverend's most devious attempt yet to envelop me within the grasp of the underworld, manipulating my feelings in such an insidious fashion. Yet I am unable to deny what I am feeling. His desperate pleas are serving their purpose. As I close my eyes, I can feel tears welling up.

"I am a good man, Anna," the reverend says. "I have always been a good man. You know this, do you not? I have worked hard to help the people of Salem, yet I have been thwarted at every turn by those who wish me harm. I took in your friend Mercy when she had no one else to care for her. I saved her from ruin and death and brought her to you. Why am I being forsaken in this way? You are my only hope. I have come here to beg you, and that is what I am doing before you now, without shame. I am begging you, Anna. I need you. You are my last hope."

His voice now sounds exactly as it once did from the pulpit. His exhortations are indistinguishable from the many sermons that he delivered on meeting days when he once implored us to stay on God's chosen path. As I open my tear-filled eyes, I notice that his desperate and anguished face is now properly arranged and the flames atop his head have been extinguished. He looks as fine and handsome as he always has. Our great reverend is beseeching me to do what has always been intended for me to do.

"I will not stop begging you," he says. "I will not leave you so easily. I will never leave you. Please, my dear and merciful Anna, you are my last hope in this world. You are all I have left."

As the reverend's anguished pleas continue, I notice that he is shrinking before me, his desperate cries slowly slipping into the ether. As he fades away, I feel myself drifting off into my own uncontrollable slumber, my cheeks stained with the tears born out of his sufferings.

CHAPTER 23

You will hunt down your enemies. You will kill them with your swords.

—**Leviticus 26:7**

Our Father, which art in heaven,
Hallowed be thy Name;
Thy kingdom come;
Thy will be done
on earth, as it is in heaven:
Give us this day our daily bread;
And forgive us our trespasses,
as we forgive them that trespass against us;
And lead us not into temptation,
But deliver us from evil;
For thine is the kingdom,
the power, and the glory,
For ever and ever.
Amen.

The gathering has gone silent at Burroughs's slow and careful recitation of the Lord's Prayer while he stands upon the cart with the noose wrapped tightly around his neck.

There is shock, of course. Many believe that a witch should not be capable of reciting the prayer. Even the hangman pauses after Burroughs had uttered his "amen." Yet I had anticipated as much from this man, and I do not retain such backward thinking.

"He is the devil!" I shout to break the stunned silence that has engulfed the proceedings. "Do not believe this trickery!"

My anger boils at their silence. How can they be so easily duped? Is this why we have found ourselves in such circumstances? Amid the shock that has overwhelmed the gathering, Reverend Mather, who has come from Boston to witness justice being carried out upon Burroughs, raises his hand to signal his desire to speak, and stands up in his stirrups upon his horse. After a few moments, the men take notice of the reverend, and begin to peer up at him to hear what he has to say.

"Gentlemen," Reverend Mather begins in his boisterous voice, well suited to be heard across the expanse of a vast meetinghouse. "It must be understood that the devil is a devious and wretched being whose sole purpose in this world is to deceive us. He goes about his work daily, toiling endlessly at this task."

Those gathered, including George Burroughs himself, appear to be transfixed as they listen to this sage speak.

"It must even be said, I am sorry to say, that the devil has often been transformed into an Angel of Light." The reverend raises his right hand above his head and moves it in a sweeping motion, as if replicating the arc of the sun across the sky. "I must say to you, gentlemen, that it is this trickery we have just witnessed before us."

There are several gasps at Reverend Mather's statement, then many in the crowd turn their gaze toward Burroughs who, disheveled and unshaven, is staring wearily off into the middle distance.

"This man has been rightfully condemned," Reverend Mather continues. "You must know that he is no longer ordained by God and, instead, he stands before you as a rightfully convicted agent of the devil."

The murmurs quickly turn to shouts, with the vitriol now directed firmly at Burroughs upon his cart.

"This man's recitation of our Lord's Prayer is trickery in the highest order," the reverend says as he jabs his index finger toward Burroughs. "Moreover, his actions are a clear indication of his guilt."

There is a roar of approval at Reverend Mather's final words, and Mather sits back down in his saddle, a scowl on his face. As he does, the hangman busies himself with his responsibilities of preparing Burroughs for his fate.

It seems we will not be fooled so easily, after all.

"Anna, why do you not say anything to me? Why do you ignore me despite the efforts that I have made on your behalf for so long?"

The Black Man's voice does not originate from his mouth, but instead seems to somehow implant itself within my consciousness. His words are delivered with great sincerity, even if I should know better than to believe such a thing.

"We have become close, you and I," he tells me. "Perhaps we might even be considered friends. Thoughts can pass between us even without words being spoken. Do you understand that I am here to help you? You can answer truthfully. All I have ever wanted from you is the truth. You should always tell me what you are thinking. There is no need to pretend with me, as you do with the others."

There is a brief silence between us before the Black Man continues.

"You are not like the others," he says in a quiet tone. "But that is a very good thing. In fact, that is why I like you so much. That is why I have been here with you for so long."

I remain entirely still upon my bed as I listen to his words in my head.

"I am sorry you are frightened of me. I am sorry you find my dark appearance so unseemly. I hope you understand that it is not my intention to scare you, Anna. That is not why I am here with you."

After a brief pause, the Black Man continues. "I have come only to help you, my dear. And you will soon see that my appearance is of no concern where we are going. My darkness is a badge of honor there."

CHAPTER 24

A wicked scoundrel digs up evil, and his slander is like a scorching fire.

—Proverbs 16:27

"If you dare touch anyone in my household with your foul lies, you shall answer for it!"

Without so much as a greeting first, my half-brother Joseph screams at my unsuspecting wife as soon as she opens the door of our house to him. Upon sustaining his sudden and venomous attack, Ann races from the room without a word. She is an easy target for a weak man like Joseph—and weak men are always quick to pounce upon those who are easy prey.

"You will not speak to my wife in that manner!" I retort loudly, waving a finger in his face. "You have come here so that we may have a civilized conversation, and the two of us will speak like men—like brothers. I will not allow you to threaten my family."

My words seem to calm my fiery sibling, at least for the moment, and he takes a seat at the table. I have invited Joseph to our farm so that we might talk through our differences. Perhaps it is too much for me to expect that we will reach a truce, but since the witching began last spring, he has been a strong opponent of the justice we are seeking. He remains, as ever, a thorn in my side.

"Let us not pretend that you are like a brother to me, Thomas," Joseph says. "You are no more akin to me than some savage Indian. If I am telling the truth, I fear what you and your family might be capable of doing to mine and my own. You and your wife and daughter seem to be seeking vengeance of some kind, and I am quite aware of my poor position within your hearts."

"We are seeking nothing more than justice! Perhaps you are unaware of what that means. Our only desire—and we are not alone in this desire, I might add—is to condemn those who do harm to others in the devil's name. It is true that I do not have a brotherly manner with you, Joseph. And I do not approve of how you go about your life. Yet that does not mean I believe you are an agent of the underworld. Can you not see the difference?"

"I see that you are drunk with power," he says in response. "You and your wife and your child have accused more than a hundred poor souls. When will it end? Tell me. How many is enough for you? Have you seen enough necks snapped at Proctor's Ledge or are there more to come?"

"So, they are victims to you?" I ask. "Is that it? Why not have a word with our new governor, then? If you do not like what is happening here, why not take it up with him? The governor has sanctioned the court and put the judges in place. I am not the one who has done those things. I am simply helping to administer the justice this community is rightfully seeking. But let me say it is truly no surprise to me that you do not have the stomach for such business, Joseph."

"Ah, I see. You believe it is proper to take someone's life on the mere word of a nine-year-old child who has claimed to see their ghost? Is that the way you wish to seek justice?"

"Have you not seen the fear in their eyes? Shall I retrieve Anna for you and show you what she looks like? Have you not seen her and the others walking about in their cruel daze? This is not the mere word of children, Joseph. It is an evil hand upon us."

"I know that you despise me," Joseph says, changing the subject. "I know you have hated me since the moment I was born—since the moment I was conceived, even." He breaks into a sly smile now and his eyes focus intently upon me. "I know that you wanted me to die when I was a child. I can imagine how you must have prayed to God to carry me away so that you might retain your precious inheritance from Father: Take him away, dear Lord, I can hear you plead. How do you think this made me feel? A child, scorned by his older brother? You were meant to be a model for me, but you never gave me a chance. And you never will."

"What do my feelings for you have to do with what is happening here right now?" I ask to redirect our conversation back to the matter at hand.

"Do you know that I keep horses saddled up—fed and watered—at all times of the day and night? I must do so, Thomas." Joseph's voice is eerily calm now. "It is so that we may flee at the first sight of the marshals, because I know it is only a matter of time. It is only a matter of time before you make your accusations against me and my family, before your wife or your daughter claim that my specter has harmed them in some unseemly manner." Joseph utters the word *unseemly* in a drawn-out fashion. "This is your chance to take your long-sought revenge against me, and I know that you will not allow it to slip through your fingers."

"What do you think we are doing here?" I ask through gritted teeth. "This is not some petty sibling squabble. This is serious business." I take a breath before continuing. "I know you do not trust Reverend Parris, Joseph. But Reverend Mather and Reverend Hale, and many others, will tell you the same thing I am telling you now. We are at war. This is a gruesome and wicked business, the likes of which we have never seen before, and we must fight against it with all our might. We must fight as hard as we have ever fought before. I know you are not used to such responsibility."

"Ha! There you go again with your duty and honor," Joseph replies with a laugh. "Do not forget that I was at Ingersoll's too, for those first examinations. I wanted to understand what we were dealing with, just as you did. I was as frightened by them then as you are now."

Joseph seems to turn introspective and then grins, as if he has reached some momentous conclusion that he relishes the opportunity to share with me. "I listened to Tituba, too," he says slowly. "I took careful notes about what she said. I have read and reread those notes many times." Joseph now turns his head and gives me a sideways glance before asking, "Did you not recognize how she told the magistrates what it was that they wished to hear from her?"

"What are you saying?"

"If you and your Reverend Parris were really listening to what these women are saying, you would realize that you know *nothing* about what is happening here. You are only hearing what you wish to hear, just as the magistrates heard what they wanted to hear from Tituba." Joseph continues as if he is a teacher scolding his pupil. "It is the devil that is whispering into your ear, Thomas," he says with a knowing look upon his face. "And he is asking you to tear us into shreds."

I am tending to my younger siblings, Deliverance and Ebenezer, when Mercy comes into the kitchen with a basket of eggs she has collected from the chicken coop. Mopping her brow with her bonnet, she appears damp and flushed from the early morning heat.

"It is warm today, my dear," Mercy tells me in her typically bright tone. "Mind yourself in the heat."

After a moment's rest, she rises from her chair and leaves without a word to tend to the vegetables in the garden. I then hurry the children outside so they can busy themselves feeding the chickens and gathering small twigs for kindling. There will be no rest for any of us today, regardless of the heat. I am feeling better than I usually do, and I am determined to accomplish my chores.

As I search for a bucket to collect water from the well, I am startled by an unusual squeaking sound that seems to break through the constant hum of chatter that keeps me company now. I cannot make out where the sound originates from, but I quickly dismiss it so that I can get on with my work.

Locating the bucket on a shelf, I hear the squeak again. This time, it is louder and more pronounced. Is it an animal? Perhaps a mouse? Trying not to be concerned, I move toward the door, hoping to open it and call for Mercy so that she might help me. As I am about to turn the door handle, I suddenly hear the unmistakable cry of a baby.

"Mother?" I call out in a meek and trembling voice, wondering if she might be nearby with my infant brother, Timothy. There is no response. I call out again, this time a bit louder, but still there is no reply. It seems that nobody is around. After a few seconds of silence, I hear the baby's cry again, but this time it rings out as clear as day in my ears.

"Who's there? Mercy, is that you?"

Again, there is no response, and I continue to hear the cries of an infant coming from somewhere inside the kitchen. I wonder for a moment if I could be wrong. Perhaps the noise is like all the other sounds that have been originating from my consciousness these past months. Perhaps it only exists within my own mind.

I vow to remain stoic and carry out my chores. Grasping the handle of the bucket and beginning to lift it, I am struck by how heavy it is. The bucket seems to contain nothing but some small pieces of cloth at the bottom that I use for cleaning, but it is considerably heavier than I expect it to be. Surprised, I reflexively release the handle from my hand and the bucket crashes to the floor with a great clamor. As it does, the loud cry of an infant rings out from inside the bucket.

I listen to the cries for a few seconds more, frozen and unsure of what to do next. Then, as the wailing becomes increasingly intense, I gingerly lift the cloth from the bucket to reveal the helpless figure of my deceased infant sister, Sarah.

I gasp at the sight of her. God took Sarah more than two years ago, at the age of six months. How can this be possible? I force myself to take another look in order to confirm my discovery, and I notice the same dark marking that Sarah had behind her ear, as well as the same ivory complexion. It must be Sarah, I think. It could be no one else.

I steel my nerves and reach into the bucket to gather the poor infant into my arms, but I am unable to move her. She seems to be pinned somehow to the bottom of the bucket. I struggle for a moment to unfix her, but it is no use. Sarah continues crying, louder than before, and I am unable to help her.

With Sarah's anguished cries ringing loudly in my ears, I lean down close to the bucket and see her small eyes staring intently back at me. "It's all right, Sarah," I say in as calm a voice as I can muster, just as I had done when she was living. "There, there, my child. It will be all right."

To my surprise, Sarah begins to calm down. Soon, her cries are nothing more than a meager whimper. As I continue comforting her, my mind begins to drift to those days after she had just come into the world, before God took her away from us. Could I have protected her from her fate? Could I have done more to ensure she had a chance in this world?

Lost in my web of tangled thoughts, something strange seems to catch my eye on Sarah's body. I take a closer look to try to make out what it is. As I lean closer to her and maneuver her a bit for a better look, I can see it clearly. A small script across the upper portion of her back reads:

ANN PUTNAM WILL PAY FOR MY DEATH

The words—so neat and tidy—appear to be written in blood. Seeing this, I gasp, and my surroundings turn entirely to black.
"Anna! What has happened? Are you all right?"
I blink my eyes rapidly when I recognize Mercy's voice, and after a moment or two, I realize I am sprawled out across the kitchen floor. Mercy is standing above me with a concerned look on her face. A bucket lies nearby, on its side, beside what seems to be dozens of thick wax candles spilled out across the floor.
"You dropped the candles," Mercy tells me when I am conscious enough to understand her. "Were they too heavy for you in that bucket? I knew you were trying to do too much, my dear. We must get you to bed at once."

CHAPTER 25

The prudent see danger and take refuge, but the simple keep going and pay the penalty.
—Proverbs 27:12

It is a strange and unusual punishment. One cannot deny that fact. And it is all the stranger for being deployed upon a man of eighty-one years, as Giles Corey is.

"These are unique times, Thomas," Sheriff Corwin tells me when I inquire about his plans for bringing the old man to heel. "It is what we prescribe for those who will not enter a plea. And so it must be," he says in his typically unfeeling tone.

I say nothing in response, but I have a strained look upon my face.

"Do not be concerned," Sheriff Corwin reassures me with a hand on my shoulder. "Corey cannot possibly hold out for long. The technique will serve its purpose."

It is said to be a punishment that dates back more than four centuries. I daresay that it has rarely, if ever, been used in Salem. Yet Sheriff Corwin shows no sign of hesitation about deploying such a method with his prisoner.

"You understand, the new charter requires that we ratify a new judicial process, which we have not yet been able to do, given the time such a task will take," the sheriff explains. "Because of this, we are in an ambiguous situation when it comes to employing methods of coercion. Until the new judicial statues are ratified, we must make do with whatever punishments we see fit to use."

It seems we are living a topsy-turvy existence now, and Sheriff Corwin's pressing technique has a role to play in our new madness. He has laid out a pallet of wooden slats and gathered a collection of unusually large boulders in preparation for carrying out old Giles Corey's punishment. Many of us have gathered to witness this uncommon occurrence. Most seem eager to see Corey's stubbornness dissolve under the pressure. My brother Edward, Nathanial Ingersoll, and some others appear anxious, twittering nervously as the sheriff busies himself with his work.

Giles Corey stands completely naked before us. His body is frail and disjointed, as if a stiff breeze might be enough to knock him to the ground. The old man is gingerly helped down onto the wooden pallet by Captain Gardner, whom the sheriff has employed to carry out this punishment. Aged and infirm, Corey takes what seems like several minutes to stretch uncomfortably upon the pallet. Once he does so, Sheriff Corwin hastily orders a second pallet of wood to be placed atop the old man. As it is put into place, Corey turns his head toward the gathering of men to shield his face and provide him with a means for taking breath. Even without a single boulder in place, the old man's face appears locked into a stiff grimace as the wooden pallet presses up against his wrinkled right cheek.

"Goodman Corey!" Sheriff Corwin calls out in his most ceremonial voice, speaking more loudly than necessary. "You have been arrested on the orders of the honorable court of our sovereign lord and lady, the king and queen, and accused of the grave offense of witchcraft. As a result of these charges against you, it is your responsibility to enter a plea of guilty or not guilty." After an appropriate pause, the sheriff asks, "What say you, Giles Corey?"

The old man, still wearing his harsh grimace, would likely have had difficulty saying anything, given the positioning of the pallet upon his cheek. But he says nothing at all, almost as if he has not even heard the sheriff's question.

"Let it be known," Sheriff Corwin bellows after a few seconds of silence, "that the defendant has not entered a plea. Therefore, Captain Gardner, please proceed with your duties!"

The captain immediately springs into action. With the assistance of two other men, he heaves one of the large boulders forward from its resting place, rolling it. Then—with the effort of all three men at once—they lift it onto the pallet, where it settles just above Giles Corey's stomach.

The old man lets out a deep breath as the stone's weight settles upon him, but he makes no other sound. After a few seconds of silence, Sheriff Corwin asks again how Corey chooses to plea.

The old man holds his tongue.

"He will not give in, Thomas. You know how Corey is." I am surprised by Edward's sudden and urgent whispers into my ear, and annoyed that he has chosen to engage with me at this moment. Despite my irritation, I fear my brother's assessment may be correct. Corey is as stubborn a man as God has ever made. He does not wish to yield his property, which he will be compelled to do upon entering a plea. It seems he is likely to hold out as long as he can.

"He will give in," I say to my brother, in spite of my own skepticism. "It is only a matter of time."

Sheriff Corwin orders Captain Gardner and his men to add two additional boulders to the pallet, which they do with remarkable efficiency. Once again, Corey does not emit a single sound, save for a brief sigh, as his burden increases. Instead, he remains stoically stretched out as the wooden pallet above him pushes harshly against his frail body. His eyes are closed and his face worn by strain.

"He cannot hold out much longer," my brother says, seemingly fearful about what is to come and anxious about the thought of witnessing the unthinkable.

"He will yield soon," I say, attempting to sound certain. "I have no doubt it will be so. And if he does not, he will have none to blame but himself."

Sheriff Corwin asks Corey again how he chooses to plea, and once again, the old man remains silent.

"Gentlemen," the sheriff announces to the gathering, "the time has come to leave the prisoner to his fate. Captain Gardner will keep us abreast of the situation." Because Corey has shown himself to be uncooperative, Sheriff Corwin has no intention of being humiliated by his continued silence.

"Is this what Christians do to one another, Thomas?" my brother whispers. He sounds angry now.

"It is what justice demands," I say, annoyed. "Corey can end this punishment right now by simply uttering his plea as any man in his position must. He is a fool."

As we prepare to leave the field, and Corey to his devices, I take one final look at the old man, his body now trembling under the enormous strain of the heavy weight of the boulders stacked atop him. He may be a fool, but I cannot help but admire his strength. As I am about to turn to catch up with Edward, who has already left the scene in disgust, I hear the words. They are like heavy breaths of air being awkwardly exhaled, weak, but still mighty in their own way, their meaning as clear as day in my ears.

"More weight," Giles Corey utters as he stares straight into my eyes. "More weight."

"How could he have been so stubborn?"

"That is not for us to say, Anna," my father responds. "We will never know why Giles Corey chose to do what he has done. He had been living in the devil's grasp for so long. He was controlled by him. His thinking was warped by the underworld. We cannot be certain that he was even aware of what he was doing."

It is the manner of Goodman Corey's death that strikes me like a gale. I can hardly imagine it. How many stones did it take to manage the task? And why would he encourage such a demise?

"It could not have been an easy death," I say to my father. "Especially for such an old man."

He does not respond, and I am silent as well, lost in my own dreadful thoughts. Still, Father remains by my side, seemingly wishing to provide me with some measure of comfort, if that is possible.

"His stubbornness should be a lesson for us all," he says quietly, almost to himself. "Satan can take control of a man's life—of a man's body, even—and make him do the most unspeakable things. You have heard what Reverend Parris has said on this matter."

I can barely hear Father's words now. They are snuffed out by a constant murmur of which I cannot rid myself.

"The sheriff was only doing his duty," my father seems to be saying. "He could not have expected such an outcome. The result is entirely Corey's own doing. He has done this to himself."

To think of what men can do to their fellow man. Human beings seem to be able to draw from a limitless pool of degradation. While we celebrate our mercy and grace as the hallmarks of our service to Christ, we remain wholly capable of engaging in the most brutal savagery when it conveniently suits our needs to do so. Have we become savage because of the world in which we live? Or is this who we have always been?

PART 3

THE RECKONING

CHAPTER 26

Do not be overcome by evil but overcome evil with good.

—**Romans 12:21**

SEPTEMBER 30, 1692

Dear Dr. Bateman,

I hope this letter finds you well.

As you have no doubt heard by now, we have been managing a fiercely difficult matter in Salem these past months. I can assure you, sir, as a prominent member in good standing within this community, that we now have the situation well in hand. You can be certain, thank God, that these wicked happenings will soon be behind us.

I am writing to you, however, about a circumstance that is less sanguine. Unfortunately, my eldest daughter, Ann, has, by all indications, been afflicted by the devil's hand these several months past. I am most grateful that God has blessed her with exceptional piety and a sturdy disposition. She is not given to weakness of mind, body, or spirit in the least.

It is my understanding that I have the honor of addressing a man of medicine who is among the few who regularly treats such maladies. As I understand it—and do not hesitate to correct me if I am misrepresenting your experience—you have had some success in your efforts to attenuate such conditions. If I am indeed correct in my beliefs on these matters, my dear doctor, then I humbly beseech you regarding my daughter's condition.

Might you be willing to travel to Salem to examine Ann at your earliest convenience? Of course, I will be most willing to remunerate you for your efforts. I am most anxious to gain your knowledgeable opinion on her condition and to be enlightened as to what remedies might be available as a means for a cure.

I will eagerly await your reply, sir, and pray that you will have good news to offer.

I am your most obedient servant,
Sergeant Thomas Putnam
Salem Village, Mass.

I have forgotten what it feels like to be alone, to be by myself with my own thoughts. A tangle of specters constantly floats nearby now, night and day. Some remain on the periphery and others are impossible to ignore. I suppose I have learned how to abide them now.

"It is me, Anna."

Father has come into my room again. He believes I am sleeping, but I find it difficult to sleep now. I am only able to do so in fits and starts. I am awake, as I often am when he comes to me, but I am resting as quietly as I can with my eyes closed. In truth, there is little difference for me now between consciousness and sleep.

My father sits on a small chair positioned next to my bed. He seems to appreciate this time with me. Perhaps he even looks forward to it. He often brings me bread and tea, knowing that I will consume them when I wake. He speaks to me in a surprisingly tender voice. Sometimes he will even stroke my hair gently as he talks, bushing it away from my face with a careful hand. It is one of the few pleasures that remain for me.

"How are you, my dear?" he asks rhetorically. "I hope you are at ease."

I keep my eyes closed tightly as he speaks, not daring to move even an inch. I pretend I cannot hear him because

I know he will speak more freely that way. He will say kind words that he would never say if he knew I could hear them.

"I have written to the doctor I told you about," he tells me. "He is in Boston. Dr. Griggs informed me about him. Griggs says this doctor might be able to help you."

I am surprised to hear this news, given that most doctors shun those in my condition. I am also aware of Father's ill feelings toward doctors. I am all the more grateful to him for not giving up on me.

"They say you are in God's hands, Anna," Father says. "Even Reverend Parris tells me that now. I have been surprised by his demeanor. He seems to be beaten. But I am not giving up on my daughter." His voice seems to have a quivering tone. "You have your life ahead of you, my dear, and it is my duty to ensure that you will live it well."

We know that God, in His infinite wisdom, is capable of the greatest miracles. But we also know He does not always answer our prayers. He did not answer our prayers for Sarah. One can never know, but it is difficult for me to imagine being released from this madness now. It seems to be a part of me.

"You are strong, Anna," Father continues, caressing my hair with his soft touch.

There are some here who do not believe me. Their sympathy drains away as my condition lingers. Father has told me so during his nocturnal visits, although I doubt he would have said anything if he had known I could hear him.

He says they have accused me of being affected, of telling lies. They say that I and the other girls are engaged in some great fantastical performance. But why, I ask, would I choose such a difficult path? If only they knew the pain and horror I have endured, they would not question my feelings.

When I am well enough, Father likes me to go to court so that I may testify against the accused. I do not like being in court. It is filled with spectators whom we do not know, people who do not live in Salem. They are here to see me and the other girls who have been afflicted. Our story has traveled far and wide now, and we have become a form of entertainment. These people do not seem to have a shred of concern for the justice we are seeking in God's name. When I look into their eyes, I can see only bitterness.

"What is it you see, Anna?" my father will sometimes ask me in a pleading whisper. "What is inside your consciousness?" Yet I know he does not expect an answer from me. I suspect he would not even want to know the answer if I could give him one.

I had once thought it impossible, but I seem to have become accustomed to this existence now. The specters are not as they once were. They do not harm me, at least not in a physical manner. I am witness to a great many fanciful things. Collections of verdant plants and exotic animals in rich colors present themselves before me with regularity. Their only desire, it seems, is to be seen.

There is a clever little fox who wears a coat of bright green fur. There are the most vibrant dandelions, resplendent in their reds and blues and purples. There is a vast rainbow of fiery colors that shines brightly above me. Playful little birds and insects dance about and sometimes sing me to sleep. There are countless bewilderments before me now. I am grateful for each one of them.

"I cannot lose you, too, Anna," my father says, in a quiet whisper now, almost to himself. "You are the best of us, my dear."

I often see Mother in this strange world, too. Yet the vision I see of her is not how she is today, but as she once was, when I was a small child. I see my mother as she was when she was free and light and full of promise. When she comes to me in this world of vivid colors, I am taken aback, overcome with emotion and unable to speak. It seems Mother feels the same way. We admire each other from a distance, through our smiles and our eyes drenched with tears. I can feel her emotions, even without words, even from a great distance. When she leaves, I pine to see her again. I vow that next time, I will approach her. I will speak to her. I will tell her how much I love her and how much I have always loved her. Yet I know I will not have the courage to do so when the time comes. I know I will smile through my tears again and pray *that she hears me, pray that she knows I love her, and that I have always loved her.*

"I am sorry, Anna," my father says. "You do not deserve this, my daughter."

"I am strong, Father," I tell him without speaking, hoping my silent words might somehow release him from his anguish.

CHAPTER 27

But whoever has doubts is condemned if he eats, because the eating is not from faith. For whatever does not proceed from faith is sin.

—Romans 14:23

I am in an impossibly dense forest, the midday sun obscured by a thick canopy of trees. I am being pursued by a fierce, painted warrior out for blood. His face is fixed with a look of stoic determination as he relentlessly hunts me down. I am resting, for a moment, by a stream, trying to catch my breath. I know I am outmatched.

Suddenly, he is upon me again, breaking into an impossibly fast sprint in my direction. I set off as quickly as I can, running through a dense thicket of foliage and felled trees. Upon taking a step, my foot suddenly sinks deeply into the mud. In my struggle to break free, my other foot becomes trapped in the mud as well. Now, with both of my legs firmly locked up to my knees in the thick mud,

I am entirely immobilized. The warrior closes in, his knife ready to slit my throat. His eyes are piercing through me as he runs toward me, closer, closer, closer ...

"Thomas!" I hear my wife say as she shakes my shoulder roughly.

I open my eyes with a start and a quick, deep breath. It takes a moment for me to recognize that I am in my bed.

"What is the matter, Thomas?" Ann asks with great concern. "You were calling out loudly in your sleep, so I woke you. Are you all right?"

"I am fine," I reply, my mind still obscured by drowsiness and tension. "It was only a dream."

"Father," I say in a calm voice from my chair near the hearth.

"Yes, Anna?"

"I have seen something," I tell him, knowing he will take my meaning.

"Tell me what it is," he says wearily.

"It was ..." I hesitate for a moment before continuing. "It was ... Reverend Parris."

"The reverend?" Father asks with surprise in his voice.

"Yes, Father. Reverend Parris."

"I see," he says in a flat and impassioned tone, his mind clearly turning. "And what did you see?"

"It was not his specter, Father," I reassure him quickly. "It was . . . it was, more like a dream. I saw him in a dream, but he was as clear to me as you are now. My vision was so vivid."

My father nods without a word, and I continue.

"He was standing at his pulpit, in the meetinghouse. He was preaching as he always does, telling us that we must do our duty for God. He was particularly impassioned. But suddenly he stopped. The reverend stopped speaking to us and looked up to the heavens, as if God were speaking to him directly. He was listening very intently to whatever it was that he was hearing."

My father looks pained now, as if he is anticipating what is to come.

"After a few moments, Reverend Parris looked down at us again. He looked out across the meetinghouse at the gathering of people, and he broke into a wide smile."

"He smiled?" my father asks.

"Yes, Father. He smiled a big, wide smile and told us that he was sorry."

"He was sorry?"

"Yes. His exact words were 'I am sorry, my children. I have been wrong. I am sorry.'"

"He has been wrong? What does that mean?" Father asks.

"Reverend Parris then said that the Lord had spoken to him, in that very moment, when he was looking up into the heavens. The reverend said God had told him that we are wrong—that he has been all wrong. Everything we think we know about God and his kingdom is untrue."

"Anna, what are you saying?"

"I am only telling you what I have seen," I respond. "As I always do."

"Of course," my father says with a sigh. "Did Reverend Parris say anything else in this dream?"

"Yes," I reply quickly. "He told us that whoever has doubts is condemned if he eats, because the eating is not from faith, for whatever does not proceed from faith is sin. It seemed to be a verse from the Bible. He then told us again, more firmly, that he had been wrong, that he had always been wrong, and that he has guided us incorrectly as a result. Then he said he is a lost sheep and we must not listen to him."

"This was not real, Anna," my father says in a stern voice, sounding almost as if he is trying to reassure himself. "It was but a dream. You had a dream. That is all that it was."

"Yes, Father," I reply. "That is what I told you. But there was more to the dream."

"There was more?"

"Reverend Parris broke into tears, Father. He was inconsolable, and those gathered in the meetinghouse began to leave. As they did, they gave the reverend scornful looks. Some even struck him as they walked by, slapping him in the face and striking his arm with their fists. Reverend Parris absorbed their abuse without a word. He fell to his knees, wailing loudly in a heap of tears."

"This is fantasy, Anna," my father says again. "Do not concern yourself with it. You are tired from your ordeal. Your mind is tired, and it has conjured up this fantastical notion. It is of no concern to us in the least."

I nod silently back at my father.

"You should rest now, Anna," he tells me. "I will bring you some bread."

CHAPTER 28

History is the story of events, with praise or blame.
—**Cotton Mather**

"I would have relished the opportunity to have been present," I say. "The ministers in their flowing black robes, their frail bodies seemingly engulfed by impending darkness."

"A murder of crows," Nathaniel Ingersoll responds with a chortle.

Edward is with us, too, at Nathaniel's ordinary, as we discuss the news of the court. It seems those with power in this province have chosen to weaken us.

"I am sure that Reverend Mather must convene these ministers regularly," I say with much contempt in my voice. "Weak men brought together for his benefit, so that he might throw his considerable weight around. It is an opportunity for this so-called great man to exercise his mighty intellect before a fawning and grateful audience. I can imagine his halting, erudite inflection making declarations while his beady eyes look down his nose upon them all."

"Thomas, please," Edward interjects. "I recognize that this news is not what we wish to hear, but you mustn't resort to insults. Reverend Mather has been supportive of our cause—remember his actions at Burroughs's execution?"

"Yet Mather seems to have had a change of heart, hasn't he?" I respond. "If these men choose to spend their time slumped in chairs, affirming proclamations about that which they know so little, what are we to do?"

"They admire their own wisdom; you will get no argument from me about that," Nathaniel says.

"And they do so while affecting matters that are of no importance to them," I add. "With the slightest nods of their heads, they can move mountains. They are idle and delicate old men uttering their pronouncements in feeble voices as they sit upon their gilded chairs."

"I have heard that Reverend Mather said it would be better for ten suspected witches to escape than one innocent person to be condemned," Edward says. "It seems he and his council believe our situation has become untenable."

"You mean to say they are asking what these bumpkins have been doing making a mockery of God's laws," I reply.

"Perhaps that is indeed what they think," Nathaniel says. "Yet the dark and twisted irony of it all is that these old men likely remember little of the proclamations they make during their conclaves. They seem to be far too busy anointing others with their vast knowledge to keep track of such details."

"Quite right," I say. "Might it be possible they are unaware of the consequences of their actions? Their weak voices reverberate far and wide across our land, whether we wish to hear them or not."

"Surely they are aware of the might they wield, gentlemen," Edward says.

"And yet they wield it so recklessly," I retort. "They are drunk with power and seem to relish their opportunities to inflict pain with their judgments against us."

"It seems that when the governor returned from the frontier, he had been unaware of what we accomplished during these past months," Edward says.

"Are we not capable of managing our own affairs?" I ask.

"Of course, we are," my brother replies. "Still, Reverend Mather seems to be concerned with our quick pace, and it is his obligation to bring his concerns to the governor. They are quite close, I believe."

"It does not surprise me that Governor Phips and Reverend Mather keep each other's counsel," Nathaniel says. "They have schemed a great deal, both here at home and while they were across the sea together. Only they and God know what has busied them these past months, but we can be assured that whatever they have done will likely be less beneficial to us than it is to them."

"I have no doubt you are correct," I add. "Tell me, gentlemen, are we to be blamed for their inability to stand the heat we have caused with our strong efforts to bring about justice?"

"We will never know the moment when it happened, but they made up their minds about our fate at some point," Edward says. "It is not for us to know the details."

"At the snap of a finger they produce some horrid proclamation to accomplish the task of stabbing us in the back," I respond sharply. "All it took was a few mumbled words from these feeble men to set our destruction into motion. A whisper into our craven governor's ear and our fate was sealed with a kiss."

"They have done it purely for their own safety," Nathaniel says, "so that they may remain insulated from whatever damage they might face because of our efforts. They are neatly managing their business to preserve their own precious reputations."

"It is a coward's choice," I respond firmly. "Yet why should we be surprised by it? I suppose we should have expected such a result. We were fools to ever believe it could be otherwise."

"You are far too hot-headed, Thomas," Edward says with an exasperated shake of his head. "I agree with you both that their decision to tell the court they can no longer accept spectral evidence is a blow to our efforts, but God remains on our side. Do not forget that."

"Tell me, my brother," I ask him directly. "What evidence can there be in our case other than spectral evidence? I had been thoroughly impressed with Reverend Mather's ability to understand the intricate workings of the devil and what is required of us to defeat him. He once seemed quite capable of recognizing the way in which the underworld has aligned itself with the papists and the heathens. He appeared fully cognizant of how this dangerous triumvirate represents an existential threat to everything we hold dear in our civilized world. But I was a fool for believing he would hold such beliefs for long, or that he ever cared about anything beyond protecting his own reputation."

"Thomas, you are not incorrect about the insidious nature of the devil and his inner workings. I will grant you that. Yet, if we hope to prevail in this matter, we must go about our business with care and order, not with abandon."

"So, we have been operating with abandon, have we, Edward?" I ask in a biting tone. "If you hold Reverend Mather's proclamations so dearly, why are you not having a drink with him instead of us?"

"Thomas, please," Nathaniel interjects firmly, his usual jovial manner tucked away for the moment. "Edward is a wise man." He nods toward my brother. "I am as upset about this business as you are—incensed by it, in fact. Still, what your brother says is true. We must work harder now to ensure that justice will prevail and that we carry it out in such a manner that posterity will look favorably upon us. It will not be easy, of course, but we will do as we always have. We will do our duty in God's name."

"That is all well and good, but what are we to do, exactly?" I ask with some irritation in my voice. "Are we to let this evil run its course, unabated, until it has ensnared every one of us within its meaty jaws? Until it has driven us into the dust?"

"This is not some local squabble," Edward interjects. "It has become much bigger than that now."

"Tell me," I say. "Why was Reverend Mather once so compelled by our efforts here that he blessed the sentence of Burroughs as he stood upon the gallows? His words resulted in Burroughs's execution." I draw out my pronunciation of the word *execution*. "Why did he raise his mighty scepter then to calm our gathering of bumpkins only to turn his back on us now?"

"All men have the right to change their minds," Edward says in a calm and steady voice. "And it is particularly so for men as important as Reverend Mather."

"Ah, so he is more important than we are," I retort.

"You take my meaning, Thomas," Edward says. "Reverend Mather has much responsibility here, and the governor relies upon him."

"The governor is too reliant upon him, if you ask me," Nathaniel says.

"Is this not a question of conscience?" I ask. "Is this not a question of what is right and what is wrong? Or is it simply a matter of power and politics?"

"We should not allow a king and queen who oversee a corrupt church on another continent to have a say in the affairs of our own church, in our own land," Nathaniel replies. "The comingling of the affairs of the state with the affairs of the church goes against the precedent we have set here. This matter was settled long ago."

"Yet the governor is fearful, Nathaniel," I say. "And fear is a powerful emotion. More powerful than any settled law. Should King William's court catch wind of what is happening here, it might mean Phips's head. A man of his station is always going to be on unsteady ground, and the governor is not about to give up what he has won by sticking his neck out for our sake."

My words seem to settle our discussion. We sit in silence for a moment, alone in our own thoughts. Yet I quickly notice a pensive look upon Edward's face. He is holding something back.

"What is it, brother?" I ask, feeling irritated. "We are speaking freely here this evening. Let us have what you are hiding from us."

"I have heard from the other deacons that, since his return from the frontier, the governor has gone to great lengths to make it known he was not aware of how many convictions there have been," Edward says quietly. "I have been told that had he known the number, he would have put a stop to our efforts much sooner."

"Did Phips himself not set up the court when he first arrived here?" Nathaniel asks.

"Of course, he did," I say in support. "In fact, it seems he had been quite pleased with himself, admiring of how fleet of foot he was with his actions. It was he who ordered the court to dispatch its duties expeditiously. And that is precisely what this court has accomplished, with our assistance. The court has carried out the governor's orders to the letter, and now he has the temerity to blame them for doing so."

"I have heard the governor has cited his concern for the lives of the innocent who might be lost in the process," my brother continues, bracing for the wrath he expects from me in response to such a statement.

I choose to go easy on Edward instead of reacting as he expects. "He did not have these same fears months ago when he demanded the court's formation, did he? What did he think would happen when he set up the court?"

"I have heard more news," Edward says, and Nathaniel and I both look at him with interest.

"There have been rumors about the governor's wife," Edward says, speaking now in a whisper. "I have been told she was making curious demands of her guards while the governor was away on the frontier, that she was asking them to remain awake at all hours and report any strange sightings."

Nathaniel and I exchange curious looks, our eyebrows raised.

"That is most interesting news, Edward," Nathaniel responds with a slight chortle. "What more do you know?"

"Nothing more," Edward says, looking uncomfortable. "Only that these rumors exist."

"Are you telling us that Lady Phips might be in the thrall of the underworld?" I ask, perhaps a bit too loudly. I cannot help relishing the discomfort my question has on my brother.

"Only that there are such rumors," he responds in a harsh whisper. "It is not for me to say what the truth of the matter is."

"The governor gives our court its authority and now he has taken it away at the very moment when it might point its finger at his family," I say. "It seems Phips has chosen an opportune time to wield his power, has he not?"

"We should be cautious about making such accusations," Nathaniel says solemnly.

"Of course," I say, my voice steady. "You are correct as always. But we have not finished our fight just yet, gentlemen."

"How are you feeling today, my dear?"

As I walk into the kitchen, Mercy's usually bright greeting is dulled by the haze that has flooded into my consciousness.

"I am well," I lie, barely able to respond to her question.

"I am glad to have the chance to see you before I start my chores this morning," Mercy tells me. "I have some news to share with you."

I carefully sit down in a chair next to Mercy without a word and do my best to focus on her mouth as she speaks, hoping I do not have any trouble hearing her words.

"You understand that my time in Salem was never meant to be permanent," Mercy says in a deliberate manner, recognizing my difficulty comprehending. "And as much as I would like to stay here with you, it is best for a girl like me to make her own way in the world."

I am not certain what Mercy means by "a girl like me," but I assume it has something to do with her being an orphan.

"I have decided to go to Boston," she says quickly, as if she is trying to get her thought out as fast as possible. "I am going to live with my cousin there."

Her news strikes me like a strong winter gale, but I show no reaction to it.

"It will take me away from the troubles here," she says. "I will be able to start anew. There will be opportunities there that a girl like me cannot have in Salem."

I give no response except to stare ahead steadily, as if into some abyss.

"Tell me it is all right," Mercy says with some urgency in her voice. "Tell me you understand why I must do this."

I remain silent, trying with all my strength to repress my building emotion. Eventually, my chin begins to quiver in the silence, revealing my feelings to Mercy.

"Anna, please!" Mercy says. "I do not wish to leave you, but I have no choice. Can you see that? It is my only chance to make it in this world. I cannot stay here. I am an orphan, a troubled orphan from the frontier. I am nothing to these people. I must go. It is the only hope I have to live."

I am too tired to cry. My tears do not come. Instead, I stand up slowly, stiffen my spine as best I can, and walk out of the kitchen without a word.

CHAPTER 29

Even my close friend, someone I trusted, one who shared my bread, has turned against me.

—Psalm 41:9

"Even Jesus had to endure a devil among his disciples, Samuel. If we have learned anything these past months, it is that we cannot be complacent about those who wish us ill."

I am doing what I can to keep Reverend Parris's spirits lifted as we converse at the parsonage during one of our regular conversations. He has been low of late, and I wish to raise him up.

"When we built our Church," I tell him, "you were the man I had in mind to lead it, the purest man for the purest church."

My efforts do not seem to be having their desired effect.

"You are too poetic for your own good," he tells me. "It will be the end of you one day."

"I will not apologize for my eloquence. Or for telling the truth."

"And not for your hubris either, it seems. I hope you know that I am grateful for your gratitude and friendship, Thomas, but I am only doing my duty to God and this community. Do not overstate my role in this business."

"You forget how easily men in your station are swayed by the desires of those around them," I remind him. "Yours is not an easy position. Even you must admit as much." I pause for a moment, wondering how I might be able to ignite Reverend Parris's passion. "Have I told you about my brother-in-law, Reverend Bayley?" I ask him.

"I do not recall," he says, with little enthusiasm.

"I had hoped that he would grow into his role as our pastor, but it seems that I was a bit too sanguine about his prospects. It became clear that his heart was not in it."

"There is no shame in such a thing," the reverend responds. "This life does not suit every man."

"We kept him at his post for several years—perhaps too many years—before we finally set him free from his obligations. I was not the least bit surprised when he left the service of God altogether to become a doctor."

"The responsibilities of a church are not easy," Reverend Parris replies. "It presents many challenges."

"But ours is not just any church, Samuel. We are building something new here, something pure that is meant to live on for generations. It will be an incorruptible beacon of God's light."

"You are quite the optimist," the reverend says. "I admire you for that."

"I have always believed in my heart that God had a hand in delivering you to us. You understand what it is we are trying to accomplish here. You understand it in a way other pastors have not. It was not a coincidence that the Almighty led you here when we needed you the most."

"I am grateful for your confidence in me," Reverend Parris says, his voice flat. "But I have no business allowing such notions to go to my head. You know as well as I do that there is still much work to be done here."

"Well, rejoice in hope, be patient in tribulation, and be constant in prayer."

"I am well aware of your knowledge of Scripture." He sounds exasperated.

"As you have said before, our most strenuous efforts must be focused on defending ourselves against those who wish to tear down what we are building," I remind him. "And it seems that there are many among us who wish to do just that."

"Do not tell me about the Porters again, Thomas," the reverend says with a deep sigh.

"It is not enough for them to steal my family's wealth; now they wish to meddle with our spiritual well-being as well."

"Now you are sounding like a true man of God," Reverend Parris says. "Always concerned with what is happening behind your back."

"How can I not be concerned? The Porters have it out for me. These are not the concerns of a madman. I have every reason to be wary."

"You have nothing to fear in the Porters. This village and its chattering will be the end of us all if we allow it to be."

"You cannot remain above the fray forever, Samuel. The Porters fear having such a pious man as you at the helm of the church. That is why they have wrested control of the committee and made things difficult for you. You must know they have no desire for a true spiritual leader. Their God is made of gold and silver. Their wish is to have a minister in name only who will bless their sordid existence so that they can carry on doing the devil's work with their minds at ease. They desire a pastor who will assuage their guilt and provide only validation, not truth."

"You are allowing your imagination to get the best of you now," Reverend Parris says. "I will not refute your claim that the Porters might desire a different kind of spiritual leadership, but I believe they will come to my way of thinking in due time. It is my duty to minister to them and make it so. I do not begrudge them their successes in life, and nor should you, Thomas. They will soon see that I am not their enemy. I am certain of it."

"You are far too assured of this notion, but I cannot fault you for that, I suppose. I know that the Porters do not have the stomach to maintain control of the church committee for long, particularly in the face of such an arduous challenge as mine. And I know that you are not afraid of a fight as well."

"Who is fighting?" Reverend Parris says with more than a little annoyance in his voice. "That is not why I have come here to Salem. The Porters are as deserving of spiritual well-being as anyone else in this village, including you. I know you believe that they are my sworn enemy, and perhaps you will be proven correct in time, but allow me to go about this business in my own way."

"The Porters are far too concerned with their worldly dealings to focus on the happenings of a local church for long," I tell him. "We are assured of victory, even if you do not believe you are in a fight."

"Well, you can be certain that I will not run off to become a doctor, Thomas," the reverend says, and gives me a slight smile.

The yellow bird has come to me again. She has nested in my window. I have watched her build her nest with painstaking detail. Every twig, carefully placed. Every leaf of grass, meticulously woven. There are eggs in the nest, too. They have a pinkish hue to them, but the yellow bird does not protect them. Instead, the eggs sit alone in her nest, exposed to the elements and the dangers all around them. When the yellow bird is here, she sings her grotesque song, unconcerned about her unhatched offspring.

As I look away from the bird's nest, my brother Thomas catches my eye. I notice him standing next to the Black Man, conversing in some strange, unknown language.

"Thomas!" I cry.

He does not respond. He seems to be too immersed in his conversion with the Black Man, the strange sounds of their words running into one another like ants on a hill. Yet I can see Thomas stealing glances at me out of the corner of his eye, seemingly trying to capture my reaction to what I am witnessing before me: my younger brother in the thrall of the devil.

"You are nearly a man now." I do not know why I say such a thing, or why I feel compelled at all to keep speaking to Thomas. Perhaps I am trying to capture his attention. Or perhaps my words are being forced out of me against my will.

"You have had no choice but to grow up quickly, Thomas," I continue. "I have tried to remain strong for you, but I know I have failed."

He can hear me. I see his reaction to my words from the subtle movements in his face. He is turning over thoughts in his mind. He looks pensive. I can see how scared and vulnerable he is.

"I am sorry about Father," I say. "I have never had the courage to tell you this, but I am sorry he has been so cruel to you."

Father believes that Thomas is weak, and he believes that somehow my brother is on a path toward betraying him. Yet, like so many boys before him, Thomas only wishes to please his father. He wishes to make him proud.

"If I could only do more for you," I say.

Thomas begins to turn away from the Black Man and toward me. He moves at an agonizingly slow pace, and once he has fully turned toward me, I am struck by his size. His frame has filled out substantially, and his face is now more angular and manly than it typically appears.

But Thomas's eyes remain as they have always been: a piercing light blue. I try my best to focus on his eyes. I want to see him as I have always seen him. I want to see the sweet and tender boy who wishes only to be good and to make us proud of him.

He is looking down on me with a brooding expression that seems to be a mixture of sympathy and dread. Thomas has the appearance of someone with something important to say. The Black Man had receded behind him, blending into the shadows like a brown beetle cloaking itself upon a branch.

"Thomas, what are you doing?" I ask as sternly as I can manage in my willowy voice. "What business do you have in my room at this hour? Why are you here with him?" I ask, nodding my head toward the Black Man.

Thomas provides no answers to my questions, and I am about to ask him more when I hear the sound. At first, I think it might have originated from the Black Man or from some other unseen entity. It seems impossible that such a dreadful sound could emanate from Thomas himself. It is a deep, dark, vibrating bass that shakes the very foundation of our home. As I hear it rumbling to life again, my eyes focus squarely upon Thomas, and quickly it becomes clear that the dreadful sound is coming from his mouth.

"You are not safe, Anna," he says in a rattling and sonorous timber.

I can offer no response, struck dumb by his voice. A moment later, Thomas continues to speak to me in this beastly manner, uttering his warning repeatedly in this low and menacing growl that seems to rattle my brain.

As he continues to speak to me, Thomas's voice starts to modulate. It is almost imperceptible at first, but eventually I can hear it clearly reflecting a softer and more tender tone.

"I know what you have done," Thomas says to me now before going silent again. After a few moments without a word, he closes his eyes and lowers his head as if nodding solemnly in prayer before me. It is as if he has exerted himself to the point of exhaustion and needs a moment to catch his breath. He stands still with his head bowed before me for several more seconds, then slowly looks up toward me again. This time, he is wearing a wry smile, and his eyes, even in the darkness, sparkle like jewels.

As he begins to speak to me again, his menacing voice is gone entirely. "Don't go, Anna. Don't leave me here on my own. I cannot survive without you."

Thomas's voice is now weak and trembling, and has a high pitch like that of a small child. I find myself overcome with sadness upon hearing it. Tears begin welling up in his eyes as he continues to plead with me in his child-like voice. "I need you. Please do not leave me!"

Soon, Thomas is on his knees at the side of my bed, howling in anguish and begging me not to forsake him. Even in my numbed and confused state, his uncontrolled sobs are like daggers into my heart.

"I will never survive without you, Anna! Now that you have signed the devil's book, he will take you to hell, and when you leave me, Father will kill me. I am certain of it. He hates me, and you are the only one who can protect me from him, as you always have. Without you, I have no chance to survive. Please do not leave me! I am doomed without you!"

The desperate pleas gush from him as his tears flow like a waterfall. I close my eyes and pray to God, asking Him to send me a sign that Thomas will be all right. I plead for a sign that Thomas will live on and not be harmed by my father or anyone else, regardless of what I may have done. As I pray, harder than I have ever prayed before, my world goes completely dark.

I have no recollection of when or how my brother's tormented pleas finally subside, but as I regain my consciousness and open my eyes again, I can see that Thomas is still with me, standing now beside my bed. As my eyes come into focus, I can see that the unmistakable wry smile has returned to his lips. There is no sign of his previous distress, and the Black Man is fully visible behind Thomas, looking on with pride at the scene before him.

Thomas appears exactly how I remember him, and when he speaks to me, his voice is his usual clipped and firm tone.

"You are just like Mother," he says coldly. "You are weak and unwell, and you will be the death of us all."

Thomas pauses briefly, and then nods his head in an almost imperceptible fashion, as if he is somehow confirming to himself the truth of what he has just said. Then, he takes a step back and disappears into the shadows with the Black Man at his side, leaving behind a swirling mist of vapor that plays jauntily above me before it, too, melts away into the ether.

I have no recollection of drifting into a slumber, but I seem to wake with the sun and rise from my bed in a thick fog of exhaustion to begin my morning chores. I somehow manage to make my way through my usual tasks despite my condition. Eventually, I see Thomas fetching water from the well near the chicken coop. He is focused intently upon his task, as he always is. I approach him haltingly, unsure if he is aware of his nocturnal visit to me.

"Good morrow," he says flatly when he notices me standing nearby. After the slightest hesitation, I return his greeting as I usually do and go about my day, just as I have always done.

CHAPTER 30

I am sure they lie, at least speak falsely, if they say so; for the thing, in nature, is an utter impossibility.
—**Thomas Brattle**

"Our situation has become more difficult," I say to my wife, with a hint of bitterness in my voice. "The world, it seems, has caught wind of our efforts, and they are not so favorable to us."

Ann is seated in her chair by the hearth, warming herself against the cool autumn air. She is having a good day, although such days come less often now. Edward has informed me of a letter that seems to be making its way through the salons of our wealthy comrades. It was written by a well-to-do merchant from Boston named Thomas Brattle and sent to a papist priest in England. It seems that the letter's primary subject was our own state of affairs.

"How could this man be against us, Thomas?" Ann asks. Her brow furrowed in a manner that betrays her confusion.

"He does not even know a thing about us. We are only doing what we must to ensure our safety and our children's safety."

"It is unfortunate that we seem destined to engage in much conflict and strife. It seems even our fight against the devil is fair game for ridicule by members of a certain class."

Ann continues to look distraught by this news.

"It seems Brattle stands with the likes of Saltonstall and Mather and even Governor Phips," I say. "He is among the many now who seem to be against our efforts. It appears that it has become fashionable to take a stand against us."

"But there are so many here who are still trying to destroy us," Ann says with a look of urgency in her eyes.

"I know," I say, exhaling deeply. "But I promise that they will never harm you, my dear. I will always keep you safe."

Ann sits back in her chair and stares into the fire. I can tell she is not entirely placated by my reassurances. In truth, I am astonished at how quickly things have soured around us. It seemed only days ago we were toasting our successes, and now God has chosen to humble us in this manner. Brattle is the sort of man so many seem to admire: educated, wealthy, curious about the world, full of his own thoughts and confident in his own beliefs, unafraid to share what he knows. Men like Brattle are never concerned with earning respect. Instead, they demand it with their pomposity and persistence. They are unafraid to meddle in the affairs of others when it suits them.

"Thomas," my wife suddenly says. "What will happen to them? What will happen to the accused who are sitting in jail?"

I shake my head without a word. I do not have an answer for her. There are more than fifty accused sitting in jails awaiting their fate. Yet, since the governor has dissolved our court, they sit in limbo.

To be sure, I have not read Brattle's letter. I have no stomach for it. But Edward tells me it has made quite an impression among the scholars of Boston and among those who wish so badly to be accepted by them. He tells me that Brattle is a member of something called the Royal Society, and as part of this supposed august assembly, he regularly exchanges letters with some of the most distinguished men of Europe. Somehow membership in this society seems to have validated Brattle's concerns about our situation. It is a tragedy of the highest order.

"Can they still hurt us?" Ann suddenly asks. "Can they do the devil's bidding from their dungeon?"

"There is no need to fear," I say in a tone of forced reassurance. "We have struck at them hard, and the devil knows what he is dealing with now." Despite my words, Ann seems to realize that I am telling her what she wishes to hear. The tension is still clear upon her face.

Brattle's letter has made quite a spectacle; there is no denying that reality now. One can only imagine the overwrought passions he conveyed in his words. Feeble-bodied men like Brattle are well known for their furious scribbling, self-importance dripping with the ink on every page. Edward tells me that he painstakingly explained in detail how wrong we have been to have dispensed justice in the manner we have chosen. He has called our children liars. There is no need to expound on the myriad of vile ways that this man—unknown to any of us and unaware of who we are—has tried to expose our affairs to the world. He had wished for his letter to make an impression, and he has received what he wished for.

Edward says that every word and phrase of this man's letter amounts to a carefully produced piece of theater, designed purposely to raise eyebrows. Men like Brattle can look down their noses at us, but it will not change the fact that we are fighting for our very survival. All the intellect in the world cannot change these facts.

"What will we do, Thomas?" Ann asks me. "How will we fight the devil if they are all against us?"

It is the very question I am asking myself now. How will we fight if we have been neutered?

"We will do what we must," I tell her. "They will not stop us. Come what may."

I have been most disheartened by Governor Phips. It seems he has been well seduced by Brattle's letter. Edward believes the letter was the primary reason he has turned against us and shut down the court. He saw that the tide was ebbing against him and he did not wish to be lost at sea. I am certain that our governor's greatest fear is to appear like the bumpkin from the eastern frontier that he is in front of his high-minded friends. He must work endlessly to reassure them that he deserves his station in life.

"And the court?" Ann's words seem to come out of nowhere. "What will become of the court?"

The court is no more, I want to tell my wife. It is lost to history now, I should say. But that is not what I tell her.

"The governor will reinstate the court, my dear," I say. "I am sure of it. He has only paused our efforts for a moment, but soon the just nature of what we are doing will be fully recognized again and the court will hold its sessions as it once did. You needn't worry about such things."

I have claimed not to have read Brattle's letter, but that is not entirely the case. There is one portion that Edward shared with me. It seems to have made a particularly strong impression.

Brattle wrote: *I am afraid that the ages will not wear off the reproach and those stains which these things leave behind them upon our land.*

Are we to believe that this gentleman is so well-informed he can see the future? Is he a fortune-teller? How has he become so confident in his judgment of our actions? Perhaps I am not privy to what is fashionable in the salons of Europe, but are we to believe that the act of avenging the devil's wrath is ever to become a "stain" upon God's dominion? Perhaps it is witchcraft that has provided Brattle with this ability to gaze effortlessly into the future.

Brattle has written: *I pray God pity us, humble us, forgive us, and appear mercifully for us in this our mount of distress.*

Forgive me, but we do not need this man to ask God for His pity on our behalf. We need only for him to keep his opinions to himself and to leave us alone, to not make our business known to every papist in Europe who would go about gleefully spreading the news of our misfortune throughout the fashionable drawing rooms of St. James and Bloomsbury.

Brattle and his ilk have the upper hand now. There is no need to pretend otherwise. It is hardly possible to imagine that the pendulum will swing back in our favor. My prayer is that we have done enough and that God will ensure our survival. I pray that the devil is not the true author of Brattle's words; that Satan, in all his insidiousness, has not been able to undermine our efforts in God's name. I pray that our eyes have now fully opened to the scheming of the underworld and to the myriad ways in which our enemies—the very enemies of God Himself—work tirelessly to bring down this great experiment. I pray that our complacency is now over.

"I must speak to the magistrates, Thomas." Ann suddenly says in an urgent and clipped voice. "I must let them know what I have seen. They will be convinced by my words. The governor will be convinced by them, too. They will see that our actions have been just and that we must keep going. Please, Thomas. We must go now...."

I sit down beside Ann and lay my hand tenderly upon hers. She is agitated and anxious, but my touch can often soothe her in these moments.

"Have I told you how lucky I have been, my dear? I think about when we were young, often, and I think about how grateful I am that God has blessed us with so many years together, that we have been given the opportunity to grow old together, with my hand in yours."

My wife does not respond to my words, but I can see the hint of a slight smile breaking across her lips. It seems I have been able to get through to her, thank God. She is safe, for now. Yet I fear that I have used up all my wit in this battle. I do not have much left to give. Still, I am proud of the fight I have brought to the devil. It is a battle I would wage a thousand times over.

Father has allowed me to leave the house for the first time in weeks, and as I walk by Ingersoll's, I see Betty standing by

herself. I have not seen her for nearly a year. She looks wearier than I remember her being, but otherwise she is the same bright and eager girl. For a moment, I think about slipping away and going about my business, but she catches sight of me before I can formulate a plan, and there is nothing left for me to do but flash a weak smile and approach her.

"Good morrow, Betty," I say in a quiet voice.

"Good morrow," she says with a smile, seemingly eager to see me.

Without saying much more than our greetings, we stroll together into the forest and find our way to our usual place. It seems we've headed there without a thought, as if it were natural for us to do so. It is the place where many of us girls go to have our own time together, away from the prying eyes of the village. I find it nice to be here again after such a long absence, despite it being the place where everything began. It is nice to feel what I used to feel before, even if it is only for a moment.

"This is where we did it," Betty says, almost as if to herself.

"Yes," I say meekly, with a slight nod.

I am surprised that Betty is so free in her talk about fortune-telling, even after all that has happened.

"It was an obsession for me, I suppose," she says in a wistful manner, her eyes pointed up to the sky.

I want to know if Betty still engages in fortune-telling, but I am afraid to ask her. I am envious of the freedom she seems to possess. But then, I suppose I have been envious of Betty about many things over the years.

"When Father sent me away, I was heartbroken," she tells me, then waits for a sympathetic response.

"I am sure it was difficult for you," I say, doing my best to comply with her expectations. "How were you able to manage it for so long?"

"Captain Sewall's home is so far away and so different from everything I know. It felt like I had been sent off to a dungeon. Father gave the captain strict orders not to allow me to leave or to even have a doctor summoned to attend to me. It was dreadful!"

"I am sorry," I say, trying my best to feign sympathy. "That could not have been easy to bear."

As Betty continues to speak about her experiences at Captain Sewall's home, my thoughts drift away, meandering in all directions, as they so often do now. Then, suddenly, I heard Betty utter something about a black man, and my mind snaps sharply back into focus.

"Father has always said that the devil is capable of taking many shapes," Betty explains. "But he most commonly appears as a large and menacing figure who is entirely black from head to toe."

"Yes, I remember that, too," I say, not indicating in the least how well acquainted I have become with the Black Man over this past year.

"When I first saw him," Betty continues, "I knew immediately that it must be the devil himself and that he must be trying to deceive me. I knew exactly what I needed to do to chase him away."

"You did?" I ask. "What did you do to chase him away?"

"This Black Man told me that if I submitted to him, he would give me all I have ever wished for in the world. He said I would immediately be whisked away from my awful captivity at the captain's home to a large and gleaming city of gold, bathed in beautiful bright light."

"You must have been so frightened," I say, with eagerness in my voice.

"Not as much as you might expect me to be," she responds with great confidence. "This dark being was tempting me with the finest things. He did not try to frighten me in the least. So I was not scared, even though I knew he was the devil."

"But how were you able to avoid his evil grip? How did you avoid getting taken to the devil's lair?"

I am eager to hear Betty's response, but she ignores my question and continues to tell me more about the fine offerings that the Black Man presented to her. "Once I arrived in this city, the Black Man told me, I would be ensconced upon the most beautiful throne of the finest and shiniest gold and jewels, gleaming in the light. I would then receive the title of queen of this magical city and rule it for all eternity."

"He would make you queen?" I ask, fighting to ensure that Betty does not notice the derision in my voice.

"Yes! And my only sacrifice to gain this unimaginable bounty was to sign the devil's book. Yet once I had accomplished this simple task, the Black Man assured me that I would not face eternal damnation at all, only that I would be installed in this paradise of the underworld and would not suffer in the least."

"But, Betty, is signing the devil's book not an improper thing to do? What would your father say of such a thing?"

"Because I am the daughter of a pastor, the Black Man told me I was a great prize for the devil, perhaps the greatest prize of all. And it is because I am the daughter of a pastor that the devil was willing to pay handsomely to have me by his side. I would not have to fear him or be concerned at all about damnation."

"I see," I respond with mock enthusiasm. "What a remarkable tale!"

"That is not all, Anna," Betty responds, eager as always for more attention. "As soon as the dark man had finished making this glorious proposition to me, I responded, without the slightest hesitation and in my loudest voice, that he was a liar and that I never wished to see him again."

"You spoke to him?" I ask, throwing a hand over my mouth.

"I screamed at him," she responds. "And the Black Man was so taken aback by my forcefulness that he became terrified.

He was entirely confounded. Such opposition was apparently something to which he had been wholly unaccustomed. In fact, this strange dark being was so shaken by my response to him that he fell into a deep silence and bowed his head in defeat before me."

"And then he left?"

"After I shouted at the top of my voice: Away, you devil! You are not welcome here! He immediately turned and shuffled away from me with a whimper, never to reveal himself to me again."

"I have never heard such a tale," I say. "Have you told your father about it?"

"It is best for me not to repeat such tales to Father," she says with a sudden look of seriousness on her face.

It takes every ounce of my strength not to tell Betty that I too have screamed frantically at the Black Man, that I too had called him a liar at the top of my lungs, and that I too have tried to live my life as piously as I can. Yet my hauntings with the Black Man have not ended. In fact, they continue, still today.

But I hold my tongue and allow Betty to remain the hero of the day, unsullied by the inconvenience of tragedy.

CHAPTER 31

... yet there will not one sinner in all the reprobate world, stand forth at the day of judgment, and say, Lord, thou knowest I did all that possibly I could do, for the obtaining grace, and for all that, thou didst withhold it from me.

—**Increase Mather**

JANUARY 23, 1693

Salem Village

I do not often gather my thoughts in a diary. Yet, given our present circumstances, I find it necessary to do so as a means of demonstrating the importance of my work and the value of our actions over this past year. It is unfortunate that there are now a great many here who are reveling in their accusations against those who were only doing their duty. Therefore, I hope that my writings will offer whomever might read these words some clarity and comfort. I pray that the Almighty will bestow His grace and mercy upon me for what I have helped to accomplish here in His name.

I must convey at the outset that my means will probably strike you, my dear reader, as rather unorthodox. It must be said that I knew with complete certainty that my oldest daughter, Anna, was strong enough to endure the trial set before her. Because of this, I did not hesitate for even the slightest moment to take the actions necessary to carry out my plan. You must understand that I knew from the very beginning—from the first moments when I saw Elizabeth Parris upon the floor of the parsonage, gravely inflicted—what I had to do. I never once wavered about these important responsibilities.

It must also be clear that Anna, my daughter, was not aware of my plan in the slightest, though, had she been aware, I have no doubt whatsoever that she would have been most agreeable to it. In truth, I did not wish to burden her with the responsibility of knowing about my plan. Anna has always done what is right, regardless of what it costs her. Like her father, she believes in Salem, and in our ability to achieve what God has always meant for us to accomplish in His name. Had she known about my plan, Anna would have carried it out without a moment's hesitation for the sake of her future children and their children. Anna wholeheartedly believes, as do I, in our sacred City on the Hill. For this, I am enormously proud.

I handled the substance just as Father had shown me in the forest all those years ago. Of course, he had never intended for it to be used in such a manner—how could he have foreseen the horrors we would face? The rye produced the mysterious substance exactly as he claimed it would if grown in the manner he described. After being carefully administered through bread, it produced the desired results exactly as I expected. The strange substance effectively elucidated Anna's visions without destroying her mind or body. This substance is a remarkable and powerful one, and only God knows quite how it works. Yet He has blessed us with its remarkable powers, and therefore, I took advantage of them. I suppose there are a great many mysteries in this world that we have yet to harness.

Anna identified more than sixty of those wretched souls, and she would not have been able to accomplish this remarkable feat without my guiding hand, or without the mysterious substance that grows in the rye. Even with Anna's relentless pursuit, too many of those evildoers managed to slip through our fingers like sand.

Still, I pray that our efforts have preserved the sanctity of our great community and put us on the righteous path God has always intended for us. Perhaps you, dear reader, know the answers I will never know. One can never escape the judgments of God or history, nor can one decide when those judgments shall be brought to bear. Such noble decisions are out of our hands, yet I believe I stand upon firm ground. I do not expect to be judged by the Almighty or by posterity as anything less than a God-fearing man who chose to do his duty, as a leader among men.

Perhaps, however, in some great twist of irony, I will be the one to be judged ill-fated in this matter. Perhaps one day there will even be witches who believe they are doing God's work. Alas, I am treading on perilous ground. It is not for me to say what the work of witches is.

Ever faithfully yours,
Thomas Putnam, Jr.

I have never seen a face as bright and beautiful as Mercy's on this day. Her fresh and surprising youthfulness is bursting forth in full bloom and her smile instantly warms my heart as I open the door.

I linger in our embrace, holding her as tightly as I can for as long as possible. I am enraptured by the safety I feel in her warmth. I have not experienced something as remarkable as her arms wrapped tightly around me in a long time.

"I have missed you," Mercy says.

I am glad she is the one to speak first. I am not sure I am able to say anything now. A bubble of emotion has overcome me, and there is a lump firmly planted in my throat. My only response is an attempt to smile and another firm embrace as tears fall from my eyes. Mercy is moved, too; I can plainly see that. Still, there is much that is not being said between us.

"Are you feeling better, Anna?" Mercy asks as she pulls away from our embrace. It is the question on the lips of nearly everyone I meet these days.

"Yes," I say, hoping not to have to go into more detail.

It is true that my days are better now, clearer, but not quite what they used to be. The nights, however, still haunt me.

"How are you feeling?" I ask Mercy, hoping to direct our conversation away from me.

"I am better, my dear. Thank God for that."

I smile at this news and genuinely feel grateful for it. I have not seen Mercy in nearly four months, but seeing her now, at my home, at the place where we shared so many moments—both gleeful and awful—is almost too much for me to bear. I find it difficult to speak with my emotions getting in my way.

"How do you find Boston?" I am finally able to ask her.

Mercy smiles at my question. "It is better there for a girl like me," she says. "It is not always easy, but I am making my way and I am content."

I am grateful that Mercy knows not to ask too much about me, about how I am doing. She has always been so clever. Yet I cannot not help but wonder what she must be thinking as she looks at me with that beautiful smile on her face. Is that pity I see in her eyes? Is it shame? Perhaps it is sadness.

It does not take long before there is little left for us to say. We smile at each other, but our smiles seem somehow hollow. They seem like reflections of a past that will never return, shadows of some distinct moment that has been lost forever. My feelings for Mercy have not changed, but we both recognize that we can never be who we once were. That moment has slipped away now, like sand through our fingers.

As I watch Mercy walk away from me for the last time, I cannot help but feel a cold and dark loneliness descend. It seems to be replacing the momentary lightness that had come over me upon seeing her. I am alone again, draped in its darkness.

But, of course, I am never alone.

Epilogue

August 1706

Fourteen Years Later

> ... *that I, then being in my childhood, should, by such a providence of God, be made an instrument for the accusing of several persons of a grievous crime, whereby their lives were taken away from them.*
> **—From Ann Putnam's confession,**
> **August 25, 1706**

I am thinking about Reverend Green's sermon as I mill about outside of the meetinghouse. He is a fine orator, and he has worked very hard to bring us together during his decade with us. He is perhaps the finest preacher I have ever heard. His voice is somehow comforting to me, although it is difficult for me to understand why, exactly. I find myself appreciating meetings for the first time in many years.

Still, I cannot deny my nerves now as I stand waiting for him to collect me. He seems to be taking his time after finishing his sermon. The meetinghouse has been empty for nearly a half hour, yet I remain here alone, waiting in the summer heat.

After several more minutes, the door to the meetinghouse finally opens and Reverend Green—he is a small man who often wears an impish grin on his face—emerges into the sunlight.

"Mistress Putnam, please, step inside."

He motions for me to come into the meetinghouse, and I make my way up the steps and into the relative coolness of the building. I follow the reverend to a small room that he uses as an office to prepare his sermons.

He wastes no time getting into our business, before I can even sit down in the small chair near the door. "Am I to understand, Mistress Putnam, that you wish to become a member of the church?" The reverend asks the question with more ceremony than I would have expected.

"Yes, Reverend Green," I reply simply, unsure of what else I should say.

He nods solemnly and then looks down at some papers sitting on his desk. He seems nervous now, unsure. "You have lost both of your parents, have you not?"

I am surprised by the question and uncertain why he is asking me such a thing. The reverend offered prayers at my parents' funerals seven years ago, when they died just weeks apart from each other. He knows I am an orphan.

"Yes, reverend," I respond flatly. "I lost them both, in quick succession, seven years past."

"And you are responsible for your younger brothers and sisters, are you not?"

"I am," I respond. "Though they are mostly old enough to care for themselves now."

Reverend Green nods absently at my answer and pauses for a moment, as if he is thinking about what he should ask next. "Mistress Putnam, I consider myself a student of history," he says to my surprise, "and, with regard to your application for membership in the church, one cannot so easily ignore history."

I suppose this is how the reverend is choosing to address my illustrious past. Of course, I had expected him to bring it up in some way. How could I expect to become a full member of the church without answering for my past? Still, his manner seems unorthodox.

"As you are well aware," he continues, "our recent history in Salem has been quite unfavorable, to say the least."

I can tell that Reverend Green is choosing his words carefully. I take care to look at him solemnly, with an expressionless face, as he speaks, but I cannot deny that I am deriving a certain enjoyment from his discomfort in addressing this issue.

"You are well aware of your place in that history," he tells me in the tone of a school master. "I do not have to recount those events to you, of course, but, given your role in them, it would be expected that you offer some sort of acknowledgment as to what you have done."

I offer an almost imperceptible nod, and, after a brief pause—perhaps he was expecting more of a response from me—the reverend continues. "It will be a concession of sorts, Mistress Putnam," he says, drawing out the word concession to make it sound more hopeful. "A recognition, you might say, that our community has moved forward in the spirit of harmony and conciliation."

"Of course," I say flatly.

The reverend's face noticeably softens at my simple response. Seemingly sure now that he will face no trouble with me, his mood brightens. Perhaps he is even a bit gratified and cocksure about being the pastor who will finally coax an apology from one of us after all these years.

"In order to be permitted to take communion, Mistress Putnam, you will first be expected to provide a written statement of contrition that I will read at our meeting, one month hence," Reverend Green says. "Upon doing so, you will enjoy the benefits of membership in the church."

"Thank you," I say, genuinely pleased.

As I stand up to leave the office, he clears his throat to signal that he wishes to say something more. "Mistress

Putnam, I have worked hard to restore order here these past few years. It was no easy task, and I have prayed that this action will not release anything untoward on the people of Salem again. You must know that this community cannot endure any further hardship."

Although I am surprised by Reverend Green's strong words, I offer only a brief and solemn nod of affirmation and a weak smile in return. He needn't worry, but I cannot blame Reverend Green for his uneasiness. I have much to atone for here, far more than any one person should ever be forced to bear.

About the Author

Greg Houle is a writer and storyteller whose short stories have appeared in numerous publications. He is also the creator and host of *The Salem Witch Trials Podcast*. *The Putnams of Salem* is his first novel.

www.ingramcontent.com/pod-product-compliance
Lightning Source LLC
LaVergne TN
LVHW091709070526
838199LV00050B/2324